W9-CPE-897

Dear to Me

**Center Point
Large Print**

**This Large Print Book carries the
Seal of Approval of N.A.V.H.**

Dear to Me

Wanda E. Brunstetter

CENTER POINT PUBLISHING
THORNDIKE, MAINE

This Center Point Large Print edition
is published in the year 2008 by arrangement with
Barbour Publishing, Inc.

The text of this Large Print edition is unabridged. In other
aspects, this book may vary from the original edition.
Printed in the United States of America.
Set in 16-point Times New Roman type.

ISBN: 978-1-60285-183-2

Library of Congress Cataloging-in-Publication Data

Brunstetter, Wanda E.
    Dear to me / Wanda E. Brunstetter.--Center Point large print ed.
    p. cm.
    ISBN 978-1-60285-183-2 (lib. bdg. : alk. paper)
    1. Large type books. I. Title.

PS3602.R864D43 2008
813'.6--dc22

2008001233

To my dear friend Diane Allen, whose love for the wildlife that comes into her yard prompted me to write this story. To Gail Blundell, who, like Melinda, loves animals and is still caring for them through her job as a wildlife biologist. And to my granddaughter, Madolynne VanCorbach, who would like to be a veterinarian when she grows up.

one

Melinda Andrews hurried across the grass, eager to arrive at her favorite spot. Just a few more steps, and there it was—dappled canopies of maple, hickory, cedar, and pine towering over a carpet of lush green leaves and fragrant needles. She drew in a deep breath, relishing the woodsy scent. The sun had tried all morning to overcome the low-hanging clouds. It finally had made an appearance, and Melinda planned to enjoy each moment she could spend here.

She slowed her pace and crept through the forest, being careful not to snag her long dark blue dress or matching apron on any low-hanging branches. After a while she came to a clearing with several downed trees. *"This looks like the perfect place for me to sit and draw."* She took a seat on a nearby log and pulled her drawing tablet and pencil from the canvas tote she had brought along.

"Where are you, deer friends?" Melinda whispered.

No response. Only the flitter of leaves as the wind blew softly against the trees.

Melinda spotted a cluster of wild yellow crocuses peeking through a clump of grass. Spring was her favorite time of the year. She lifted her pencil, ready to sketch a rabbit that had hopped onto the scene, when two does stepped into the clearing.

"You're so beautiful," she whispered.

The does lifted their heads in curiosity as a hawk soared high overhead.

For the next several minutes, Melinda watched the deer nibble on leaves while she sketched their picture.

Her stomach rumbled, and she thought about the tasty lemon sponge pie Papa Noah had made last night. She'd had a sliver of it for breakfast this morning, even though it wasn't considered a traditional breakfast pie, like granola pie or Bob-Andy pie. Melinda thought her stepfather was the best cook in Webster County, Missouri. As far as she was concerned, everything he baked tasted *wunderbaar.*

Melinda was only six years old when her real father was hit by a car and killed. Shortly after his death, Melinda's mother gave up her career of telling jokes and yodeling among the English, which was how the Amish referred to the outside world. She and Melinda had caught the bus from Branson to Seymour and come to live in the Amish community with Grandpa and Grandma Stutzman.

Even though Melinda had been young back then, she remembered some things about their arrival in Webster County. She especially recalled meeting her aunt Susie Stutzman for the first time. Susie was Grandma's youngest child, and she was a year older than Melinda. She and Susie had become friends right away and had remained so ever since.

Melinda smiled at the remembrance of seeing the way her aunt had been dressed, in a long blue dress with a small white *kapp* perched on top of her head.

"Plain clothes" is what Mama had told Melinda. "My folks follow the customs and rules of the Amish church, and they live differently than we're used to living."

Melinda hadn't minded wearing the unusual clothes, for it seemed like she was playing dress-up at first. But the strange rules and numerous jobs Grandma Stutzman expected her to do were the hardest part. Then Noah Hertzler came along and started taking Melinda and Mama places—to Osborn's Christmas Tree Farm where he worked, out to lunch, to the farmer's market in Seymour, and on several picnics.

Melinda smiled. *I figured he would be my new* daed *even before Mama said she loved him.*

She lifted her face to the sun as her thoughts turned to Gabe Swartz. He had recently begun courting her. Gabe had hazel eyes with green specks and brown hair that curled around his ears. He was tall and slender yet strong and able-bodied, and she'd had a crush on him ever since they attended the one-room schoolhouse down the road.

When Gabe, who was a year older than Melinda, graduated from eighth grade and left school to learn the trade of woodworking under his dad's tutelage, she missed seeing him every day and looked forward to their every-other-Sunday church services, where Gabe and his family would be in attendance. Now Gabe was twenty years old and worked at his father's woodworking shop.

When Melinda finished school, she had begun her

vocational training at home with her mother, where she learned various household chores that would prepare her for marriage. Then a year ago, she'd started working part-time for Dr. Franklin, the local veterinarian. At first it was just cleanup work, as well as feeding, watering, and exercising some of the animal patients. But later, when the doctor realized how much she cared for the animals and that she had a special way with them, he had allowed her to assist him with minor things. Melinda had done everything from holding a dog while it got a shot, to giving flea baths and bringing animals from their cages into the operating room.

"You've been blessed with a unique gift," the doctor had told Melinda the other day while she held a nervous kitten about to receive its first shot. "Have you ever considered becoming a veterinarian or even a vet's technical assistant?"

Melinda had to admit that the thought had crossed her mind, but she figured it was an impossible dream. Not only was she lacking in education, but going to college and then on to a school of veterinary medicine would mean leaving the Amish faith and becoming part of the English world. Since she had been baptized and joined the Amish church a year ago, leaving the faith would also mean that Melinda would be shunned. She knew that each district, with its own bishop and ministers, made the decision about how harsh the shunning would be.

She remembered several years ago, before their

old bishop had died, a young man named Abner had left the faith to marry an English woman he'd met during his *rumspringa*—running around days. Abner had tried coming home for a visit a few times, but his friends and family members were not even allowed to speak to him. It was as though he were dead. She didn't know how hard her shunning would be under Bishop John, but she knew that even if she could come home for a visit now and then, she would not be allowed to eat at the same table with her family, and no one could serve her or do any kind of business with her.

It would probably break Mama's heart if I left home the way she did when she was my age. And what would it do to my relationship with Gabe? Would he be willing to become English with me? It would certainly be more bearable if we could be together.

A twig snapped from behind, and Melinda jumped up.

"So this is where you've been hiding. I might have known!"

The deer bolted into the protection of the thick pine tree forest, and Melinda spun around. There stood Aunt Susie, dark eyebrows furrowed and both hands on her slender hips.

"Thanks a lot. You've scared away my subjects, and they probably won't be back." Melinda sniffed. "Leastways, not today."

"Sorry about that." Susie didn't look one bit sorry. In fact, she looked rather pleased with herself.

Melinda stood. "I'll bet you hollered like that on purpose."

The smirk on Susie's cute round face told Melinda she was right.

"Why?"

"Because your *mamm's* looking for you, and I knew if I just whispered in your ear, the deer would stay put and you'd keep on drawing."

Melinda groaned and flopped back down on the log.

"After we eat lunch, your mamm and my mamm need our help baking pies for Sunday after church. As you know, it's going to be held at my folks' house this week."

"*Jah,* I know." Melinda slipped her drawing tablet and pencil into the canvas tote at her feet. "How'd you know where to find me?"

Susie wrinkled her nose. "You're kidding, right?"

Melinda let her gaze travel around the wooded area. "Just listen to the music of the birds and smell that fresh pine scent from all the trees. It's so peaceful here, don't you think?"

"I suppose so, although there are other things I'd rather do than sit in the woods for hours on end." Susie took a seat on the log beside Melinda. "What draws you to the animals in this forest, anyway?"

"Every animal God created is special, but the ones in the woods fascinate me more than any others."

"There's a big difference between fascinated and fanatical."

Melinda snickered. "Fanatical, is it? Since when did

you start using such fancy words?"

Susie shrugged. "I've been readin' a fiction novel about a young woman who likes to solve mysteries. Her mother accuses her of being fanatical."

"You'd better not let your mamm know you're reading novels that the Englishers like to read, or she'll become *fanatical.*"

Susie clicked her tongue. "Who's gonna tell her—you?"

"'Course not. You know I'm not one to blab anyone's secret."

"No, but you sure do like to change the subject."

"What subject was that?"

"Animals, and your great love for them."

"Oh, that."

"Ever since you were little, you've been playin' nursemaid to any stray animal that comes near your place, and I just don't understand it."

Melinda scrunched up her nose. "You think me wanting to care for animals is a bad thing?"

"I guess not, unless it's all you think about or spend your time on." Susie turned her head sharply, and a wisp of cinnamon brown hair came loose from her bun.

Melinda reached over and pushed it back in place. "I thought it was only me who didn't get their bun put up right."

Susie chuckled. "Guess that's one thing we have in common."

Melinda frowned. "What do you mean? There are lots of things we both like."

Susie elbowed Melinda gently in the ribs. "Jah—lemon sponge pies, barbecued beef, and Aaron Zook's new puppy, Rufus."

"You sure it's not Aaron you're interested in, and not his dog?"

Susie's elbow connected with Melinda's ribs a second time. "You're such a kidder."

"I wasn't kidding."

"Aaron's more like a brother to me than anything."

"Jah, me, too. His mamm and my mamm have been friends a long time. Her *kinner,* me, and Isaiah have grown up together." Melinda scanned the woods again, hoping the deer might return.

"You and Gabe Swartz have been courting a few months now. Do you think he will ask you to marry him?" Susie asked, changing the subject.

"That all depends."

"On what?"

"On whether I decide to—" Melinda jumped up, glad she had caught herself in time. It might not be a good idea to let her young aunt know what she was contemplating. Knowing Susie, she would likely blab to her older sister, who was Melinda's mother. Then Melinda would probably have to listen to a list of reasons why she shouldn't follow in Mama's footsteps and leave the Amish faith. No, she wasn't ready to discuss Dr. Franklin's idea about her becoming a veterinarian with anyone just yet.

Melinda grabbed Susie's hand and gave it a tug. "We'd better go. Don't want to keep our mamm's waiting."

• • •

Gabe whistled as he swiped a piece of sandpaper back and forth across the door of a new kitchen cabinet. He was alone at the shop today, as Pap had gone to Seymour to pick up some supplies he'd recently ordered. Knowing his *daed,* Gabe figured it might be some time before he returned. Usually whenever Pap went to town, he would head straight for a fast-food restaurant and get a juicy cheeseburger and an order of fries. Then he'd often drop by Lazy Lee's Gas Station and chew the fat with whoever was working that day.

When I'm done with this door, I think I'll start making that birdhouse I plan to give Melinda for her nineteenth birthday next month. She's always feeding the birds and taking care of any that gets hurt, so I'm sure she'd like to have another birdhouse—maybe a feeder, too.

Gabe rubbed his chin. *Hmm . . . I could even make a birdhouse that has a feeding station attached to it. I'll bet she'd like that. A* vision of Melinda's pretty face popped into his mind. Her golden blond hair and clear blue eyes were enough to turn any man's head. He'd been in love with her since they were both kinner.

The cowbell hanging by a rope on the front door jangled, and Gabe looked up.

Melinda's stepfather, Noah Hertzler, entered the room. "Hey, Gabe. How's business?"

"Doin' well enough. How's your job at the Christmas tree farm?"

"I'm keeping plenty busy." Noah looked around.

"Where's your daed? Is he around someplace?"

"Gone to Seymour to pick up supplies. Probably won't be back for a few hours yet."

Noah chuckled. "If I know Stephen, I'll bet he's havin' lunch at his favorite burger place today."

"No doubt, but I don't know why Pap would choose fast food over barbecued ribs, baked beans, or hillbilly chili."

"I have to agree, but then each to his own."

"Jah. Everyone has different likes and dislikes." Gabe moved over to the desk in the center of the room. "What can I help ya with, Noah?"

"Thought I'd see if you could make me a birdhouse. I want to give it to Melinda for her birthday next month."

Gabe inwardly groaned. There went his plans for Melinda's special birthday present. He didn't have the nerve to tell Noah he'd planned to give her a combination birdhouse-feeder. *Guess I'll have to come up with something else. Maybe I could whittle a little fawn, since she seems so taken with all the deer that live in the woods behind their place.*

"I'm sure I can have a birdhouse done for you in time for Melinda's birthday," Gabe said. "Any particular size or color you're wanting it to be?"

Noah shook his head. "You're the expert, so I'll leave that up to you."

Gabe smiled. He liked being called an expert. Most folks who came into their shop thought Pap was the professional woodworker, and many saw Gabe as merely his daed's apprentice. Someday, though, Gabe hoped to have his own place of business, and then nobody could think of him as an amateur in training.

Noah leaned against the desk and visited awhile, even after Gabe wrote up the work order and resumed sanding the cabinet door he'd been working on. Gabe wondered if Melinda knew how fortunate she was to have such a nice man as her stepfather.

Wouldn't mind having Noah for my father-in-law, Gabe mused. *That is, if I ever get up the nerve to ask Melinda to marry me.*

two

"How come we baked so many pies today?" Melinda asked her mother after Grandma Stutzman and Aunt Susie headed for home. "Won't some of the other women be bringing desserts on Sunday?"

"It was your grandma's idea to have a pie social Sunday afternoon, and she wanted to furnish all of the pies," Mama said as they finished cleaning the kitchen. She handed Melinda a sponge and pointed to the wooden table in the center of the room, where streaks of flour and globs of gooey pie filling stuck to the oilcloth covering.

Melinda gave the table a thorough cleaning, dropping the mess into the garbage can under the sink. "If church is going to be at Grandpa and Grandma's, why did we do the baking over here and not at their place?"

"Because your daed's busy with other things today,

and I didn't want to leave Grandpa Hertzler alone in the *daadihaus*—grandparents' house all day. As you know, his memory isn't so good these days. No telling what might happen if he were left by himself for any length of time."

"That's right," Melinda's eleven-year-old brother said as he came up behind their mother. "Remember the last time we left Grandpa alone when we went to the sporting goods store in Springfield? When we got home, he wasn't here, and we found him down the road at the schoolhouse." The boy snickered and pushed a hunk of dark hair away from his eyes. "I still can't get over seein' Grandpa on one of the swings, talkin' to Grandma like she was right there."

"Grandpa's memory loss is no laughing matter, Isaiah. Your daed and I are watching him closely, and if he should get any worse, we'll be taking him to see a specialist in Springfield." Mama shooed Isaiah away with a cotton dish towel. "Now get back outside and see that the rest of the wood is chopped before your daed gets home."

"Okay, I'm goin'." Isaiah grabbed a handful of peanut butter cookies from the ceramic jar on the cupboard, then headed out the back door.

"That boy," Mama muttered, as she ran water into the sink. "It'll be a miracle if I'm not fully gray by the time he's grown and married."

"If he can ever find a wife who'll put up with him." Melinda's forehead wrinkled. She thought her young brother was a bit spoiled. The fact that Mama wasn't able to have any more children after Isaiah was born could account for the fact that she didn't always get after the boy the way she should. At least that's how Melinda saw it.

"Isaiah's young yet. There's still plenty of time for him to grow into the kind of man a woman would want to marry," Mama countered.

Melinda's thoughts went to Gabe, the way they usually did whenever the subject of marriage came up. Was he the man she would marry? She cared deeply for him, but what would happen to their relationship when she finally told him that she was thinking of leaving the Amish faith to become a veterinarian? Would he think she was *ab im kopp*—off in the head— or would he understand her desire to care for animals in a more professional way?

Pushing her thoughts aside, Melinda glanced at her mamm, engrossed in the job of washing dishes. Mama's once shiny blond hair had turned darker now, and a few streaks of gray were showing through. Even so, she seemed youthful and full of energy. Mama had a zest for living, often telling jokes and yodeling when the mood hit—and whenever Grandpa Stutzman wasn't around. He often said he found yodeling an annoyance, even though many Amish in their community liked to yodel.

I enjoy yodeling. Melinda wiped down the refrigerator door, also splattered with gunk. *But I don't do it when I'm in the woods because it would probably scare away the deer.*

"Did you read your Bible this morning?" Mama asked suddenly.

Melinda sucked in her lower lip, searching for words that wouldn't be a lie. "I'll do it this evening before bed."

"I have found that in order to stay close to God, one needs to spend time with Him in prayer and Bible reading," her mother said.

"I feel close to God when I'm out in the woods or with the animals at Dr. Franklin's veterinary clinic."

"That may be, but it's not the same as reading God's Word."

"I know. I'll read some verses tonight," Melinda promised.

"Jah, okay. In the meantime, would you check on that last pie we've got baking?"

Melinda set the sponge on the table and went to open the oven door. When she looked inside, it appeared as if the lemon sponge pie was done. Just to be certain, she sliced a knife through the middle. "It's ready," she announced when the knife came out clean. "Bet it won't be nearly as good as the ones Papa Noah bakes." She pulled two pot holders from a drawer and carefully lifted the pie from the oven. "Should I turn the propane off?"

"Go ahead. I won't be needing the stove again until supper time."

Melinda set the pie on top of the stove while she turned the lever on the propane tank. She was thankful her folks didn't use a woodstove for cooking, the way some Amish in their community did. Wood cooking was too hot and could even be dangerous.

Melinda remembered once when she was young how her mother had caught the kitchen rug on fire after a piece of wood fell out of the firebox. Fortunately, Mama got the rug and chunk of wood thrown outside before anything else caught fire, but the whole kitchen had become a smoky mess. Mama's pie had been ruined, too, and Melinda had been forced to sit outside in the cold until the smoke was all gone.

Melinda picked up the pie again and started across the room. While it cooled on the kitchen table, she planned to go out to the barn and check on the new baby goat that had been born a few days ago.

She'd only made it halfway to the table when the back door flew open and Isaiah rushed into the room. "My dog broke free from his chain again, and he's chasin' chickens all over the yard!"

Before either Mama or Melinda could respond, Hector, Melinda's favorite rooster, flew into the house, squawking all the way. Isaiah's hound dog, Jericho, followed, nipping at Hector's tail feathers. The rooster screeched and flapped his wings, and the two of them darted in front of Melinda, causing her to stumble. The pie flipped out of her hands, landing upside down on the floor.

The dog halted and sniffed the lemon filling. He must have realized it was too hot to eat, for Jericho let out an ear-piercing howl and ducked under the table. Hector crowed as he strutted around the room, and Isaiah stood there howling.

"Ach!" Mama shouted. "Get those critters out of my kitchen!"

Melinda didn't know whether to laugh or cry. The pie was ruined, and Hector could have gotten hurt, but the whole thing was kind of funny. "You'd better get your dog," she told her brother. "After I clean up this mess, I'll take Hector outside and put him in the chicken coop."

"Better yet, I'll clean the floor and you can take the rooster out now," Mama said sharply.

Melinda frowned. "It wasn't Hector's fault Jericho broke his chain and chased the poor bird."

Mama tapped her foot. "I don't care who was at fault. We have one less pie now and a big mess to clean."

Melinda bent down and scooped Hector into her arms. Isaiah grabbed his dog by the collar, and they both went out the door.

"As much as I like animals," she muttered, "I have no use for that mutt of yours. He's dumber than dirt."

"Is not," her brother retorted. "Why, I'll have you know that the roof of Jericho's mouth is really dark, which means he's a smart one."

"That's probably just an old wives' tale you heard somewhere."

"Why don't ya see what the vet has to say about it?"

Melinda shook her head. "I'm not going to bother Dr. Franklin with something so silly."

"It ain't silly, and it'll prove once and for all that Jericho ain't dumb."

"I'll think about it," Melinda muttered. Didn't her little brother realize she had a lot more on her mind than finding out if the color of a dog's dark mouth meant it was smart or dumb?

When Melinda's stepfather returned home late that afternoon, she was in the barn with the baby goat.

"How was your day?" she asked as he entered the building to put his buggy horse away. "Did you get everything done that you had wanted to do?"

He nodded. "Worked the first half of the day at the tree farm, then stopped by Swartz's Woodworking Shop around noon. After that I ran some other errands."

"Did you see Gabe by any chance?"

"Sure did. He was workin' at the shop alone 'cause his daed had to go to Seymour to pick up supplies."

Melinda was tempted to ask if Gabe had mentioned her, but she thought better of it. If Papa Noah knew how much she cared for Gabe, he'd probably tease her the way he did Mama whenever she was in one of her silly moods.

Melinda continued to stroke the goat behind its ears as she thought about how sweet Gabe had been on their way home from the last singing. He'd asked if she was cold, and when she said, "Jah, just a bit," he had draped his arm around her. Melinda could still feel the way his long fingers had gently caressed her shoulder, and even now, just thinking about it caused her to shiver.

"You cold?" Papa Noah asked as he grabbed a brush and started grooming the horse.

She shook her head. "Just felt a little chill."

"Spring has been fairly warm so far, but it does cool off in the evenings," he commented.

"Jah, that's for certain sure."

"Did you and your mamm get those pies baked today?"

"With Grandma and Susie's help, we did."

"How'd they turn out?"

Melinda moved over to the horse's stall. "They looked fine, but I'm sure they won't taste half as good as those you bake." She figured there was no point in telling her stepfather about the one that had fallen on the floor. Mama would most likely give account of the whole story during supper.

He chuckled and reached under his straw hat to scratch the side of his head. "Don't get to bake as often as I used to, what with havin' so many other things to do."

"Mind if I ask you something, Papa Noah?"

"What's that?"

"What's going to happen if Grandpa Hertzler's memory loss gets worse? Will he have to move into our side of the house?"

"Maybe so."

"Sure wish there was something we could do to make him feel better."

Papa Noah's dark eyes clouded over. "We just need to remember to pray for Grandpa and be there whenever he needs us."

"Jah, I agree."

"So, how's that baby goat you were cuddlin'?" he asked. "Is she doin' all right?"

"I think so. I thought at first she might need me to bottle feed her, but her mamm seems to be takin' care of her now."

"Glad to hear it."

Melinda swatted at a bothersome fly. That was the only bad part about being in the barn—too many bugs that liked to buzz and bite. "Say, Papa Noah, I was wondering if . . ."

"What's that?"

"Do you think you might have the time to build me a few more animal cages so I can take care of any orphaned animals that are brought to Dr. Franklin and passed along to me after he does whatever doctoring is needed?"

"Not sure I'd have the time right now, but I'll bet Gabe Swartz would."

"Should I ask him?"

"Don't see why not." He winked at her. "After all, a fellow bitten by the love bug is sure to do most anything for his favorite girl."

Melinda's mouth dropped open. "You know about Gabe and me?"

"Of course. Can't fool an old man like me. I've seen the way you two look at each other."

"You're not old, Papa Noah." Melinda reached out to touch his arm. "You don't even have any gray hair yet."

25

He gave his beard a quick tug. "I've got some here, though."

She leaned in closer for a better look. "Well, maybe just a few. But I still think you look plenty young."

He chuckled. "You sound just like your *mamm.*"

"Is that a bad thing?"

" 'Course not. If you was to follow in your mama's footsteps all the way through life, it would be a right good thing."

Melinda felt the heat of a blush cover her cheeks. *If Papa Noah knew what I'm thinking of doing, he might wonder if I was preparing to follow in the footsteps Mama took when the left the Amish faith many years ago.*

three

Melinda hurried through her kitchen chores, anxious to get outside. She planned to check on the baby goat and its mother, see that Isaiah's dog was secured for the day, and make sure all the chickens were doing okay. After yesterday's close call with Hector, she didn't want to see a repeat performance, and she was sure her mother didn't, either. Mama hadn't been happy about the loss of the pie, but Papa Noah saved the day when he baked another one that evening.

"I'm going over to Grandma Stutzman's to help her clean," Mama said, as Melinda passed her in the downstairs hallway. "Your daed, Grandpa Hertzler, and Isaiah loaded the pies into the buggy and will drop them over there before they head to Ben and Mary King's place to pick up the benches for tomorrow's church service."

"Oh, that's right. Preaching was held at their home two weeks ago."

"Jah."

"I'm glad Grandpa won't be left home alone, because I'll be heading for work soon."

Mama popped a couple of her knuckles, a habit she'd had ever since Melinda could remember. "I didn't think you'd be working today. Thought it was just Monday, Tuesday, and Thursdays you helped out at the veterinary clinic."

"It was, but Dr. Franklin thought I could learn some new things if I spent more time there, so I may be working some Saturdays, too."

Her mother released a sigh. "Learn more of what, Melinda? I thought you were just hired to clean the cages and feed the animals."

"I was, but sometimes the doctor lets me do certain things—like give a dog its flea bath or hold on to a nervous cat while he's examining it." Melinda shrugged. "He says the animals are calmer when I'm there."

"Jah, you do have a way with animals, even the unruly ones like Hector."

Melinda opened her mouth to defend the poor rooster and remind her mother that the incident yesterday was Jericho's fault, but Mama grabbed her black purse off one of the wall pegs and headed out the door. "See you this evening. Have a *gut* day."

"You, too."

Melinda stood in the doorway watching her mother head down the driveway on foot. Since Grandpa and Grandma Stutzman lived less than a mile away, Mama often chose to walk there instead of bothering with a buggy.

Melinda smiled at the way her mamm held her head high, with shoulders straight back and arms swinging in perfect rhythm with her long legs. Soon Mama began to yodel. "Ohlee-ay-tee—oh-lee-ay-tee—oh-lee-ay-tee-oh!"

Melinda cupped her hands around her mouth and echoed, "Oh-lee-ay-tee—oh-lee-ay-tee—oh-lee-ay-tee-oh."

Mama lifted her hand in a backward wave, and Melinda shut the door. She needed to get busy and clean her room before she left for the clinic. Then, if there was enough time, she wanted to check on the animals in the barn.

For the next half hour, Melinda dusted, shook her oval braided throw rug, pulled the colorful crazy quilt up over the four-poster bed, and swept the hardwood floor. When she finished, she noticed her writing tablet on the dresser, and it reminded her that she'd forgotten about the note she was supposed to leave Gabe inside the old birdhouse near the front of her folks' property. She grabbed a pen from the drawer and hurriedly scrawled a message.

Dear Gabe,

I got your last letter, and jah, I do plan on going to the singing tomorrow night. In answer to your other question—I would be pleased if you were to give me a ride home afterward.

I've enclosed a picture I drew of the baby raccoon Ben King found in the woods behind his place the other day. He said the critter's mother was killed, so the poor thing needs a home. I told him I would keep her, since the coon seems to have a problem with her eyes and probably wouldn't survive on her own. I've named her Reba, and I can't wait for you to see her.

I look forward to seeing you at church in the morning. After the common meal, maybe we can play a game of croquet with some of our friends. Until tomorrow . . .

Yours fawnly,
Melinda

Melinda slipped the note, along with the picture of the orphaned raccoon, inside an envelope and hurried out of her room. She made a quick trip to the barn and was pleased to discover that the baby goat was sleeping beside its mother. The kid's bulging tummy let Melinda know it had recently eaten, and for that, she felt a sense of relief. Too many times Melinda had bottle fed some animal because it was orphaned or its mother wouldn't take care of it.

"Sleep well, and I'll check on you again after I get

home from work this evening," she murmured.

Melinda led her favorite buggy horse, Jenny, out of the barn and hitched her to one of their three open buggies. Sometimes she wished they could drive the box-shaped, closed-in buggies most other Amish communities used, but when she and Mama first moved to Webster County, Mama had explained that the community she belonged to was more conservative than most. One of the things they did that separated them from other Amish was to drive only open buggies.

"These buggies aren't so bad in warmer weather," Melinda murmured, "but in the wintertime, it sure can get cold." She gave Jenny a quick pat, climbed into the driver's seat, and picked up the reins.

At the end of the driveway Melinda saw the familiar gray birdhouse, and she halted the horse. "Just a few more minutes, Jenny, and we'll be on our way."

She hopped down and lifted the removable roof from the birdhouse. She was pleased to see that no birds had claimed it as their new home. She and Gabe had been sending each other messages this way since they'd started courting a few months ago, and so far the birds seemed to know it was off-limits.

She slipped the note inside and replaced the roof. "I just hope Gabe comes by before tomorrow and picks it up."

Melinda was about to walk away when she caught sight of a small bird in some tall grass, chirping and furiously flapping its wings. She bent for a closer look and realized it was a fledgling blackbird that apparently couldn't fly well yet.

"I can't leave you here. Some big cat or hawk might come along and make you its meal." Gently, Melinda picked up the tiny bird and set him on a low branch of a nearby tree. "There you go; be safe." She smiled and hurried away.

Gabe shielded his eyes from the glare of the sun and pulled his buggy to the side of the road by the Hertzlers' driveway. *Sure hope there's a note from Melinda today.*

He hopped down and lifted the lid of the weathered birdhouse. To his surprise, there were a few blades of grass and a piece of string lying on top of an envelope. "Some bird must have decided to make a nest here," Gabe muttered. He reached inside, pulled out the grass and string, and tossed them on the ground. "That ought to discourage those silly birds."

Unexpectedly, a sparrow swooped down, just missing Gabe's head. He ducked. "Hey, cut that out! This is Melinda's and my message box. Go find someplace else to build your nest."

Gabe quickly stuck his hand inside the birdhouse and retrieved Melinda's note. As soon as he had replaced the lid, he bent down, grabbed a small rock, and plugged the opening in the front. "There, that should keep you birds out of there."

As Gabe climbed into his buggy, he made a decision. In all fairness to the birds, it wasn't right to shoo them out of a birdhouse that was really built for them. So he would add a separate compartment to the birdhouse he was making Noah to give Melinda for her birthday. Then, even if the birds decided to make it their home, he and Melinda would still have their secret place to hide messages—one without a hole in the front.

Gabe headed down Highway C toward Seymour, letting the horse lead while he read Melinda's note. He was pleased to discover that she planned to be at the singing tomorrow night and was agreeable to the idea of him taking her home afterward.

"I like a woman who knows what she wants," he said with a chuckle. "Especially if it's me she's wanting." Her eagerness to be with Gabe made him believe she might say yes if he were to propose marriage.

He studied the pencil drawing Melinda had made of the baby raccoon. It was well done and certainly looked like a coon. But he couldn't help feel some concern about her making a pet out of a wild animal. What if the critter bit or scratched her real bad? She could end up with rabies or something!

"That woman doesn't think straight when it comes to the animals she takes in," he mumbled. "I believe she'd cozy up to a bull snake if she thought it needed a friend. Maybe I should have a talk with Melinda and let her know I'm concerned."

four

On Sunday morning, when Melinda and her family arrived at Grandma and Grandpa Stutzman's for church, Melinda spotted Susie on the wooden two-seater swing hanging from the rafters under the Stutzmans' front porch. Papa Noah and Isaiah headed to the barn to put the horse inside, and Mama and Grandpa Hertzler went into the house right away. Melinda stopped at the swing to see Susie.

"I'm surprised you're out here and not inside helpin' your mamm get things ready," she said.

"We've got the meal prepared for after preaching. Besides, Faith just went in, and since she and my other two sisters are there, if there's anything else to be done, I'm sure they'll take care of it." Susie stopped swinging and patted the seat beside her. "Sit with me awhile before everyone else shows up."

Melinda sat down and started pumping her legs to get the swing moving again. The temperature was warmer today than most other April mornings had been this year, and the breeze from the motion of the swing felt nice.

Susie glanced over at her and frowned. "I see you've got dark circles under your eyes. How come?"

"I stayed up late last night caring for my animals."

"Which ones?"

"I've only got a couple right now. I checked on the baby goat to be sure its mother was still feeding her, helped Papa Noah groom the horses, and spent some time with my orphaned raccoon because she was acting kind of peculiar."

"What coon?"

"I got it from Ben King. Reba's an orphan, and she's nearly blind."

"That's too bad."

"At first she wouldn't eat and kept bumping into the side of her cage. After I sat with her awhile, she finally ate a little and seemed much calmer."

Susie groaned. "I can't believe you'd lose sleep over some dumb critter, or that you'd even bother to name a wild animal."

"Reba's not dumb. Do you think your cat's dumb?"

" 'Course not. Daisy's a good mouser. She also keeps me company and likes to cuddle."

"Well, there you go."

"Are you still planning to go to the singing over at the Hiltys' place tonight?" Susie asked, taking their conversation in another direction.

"Sure am." Melinda smiled. "Gabe's giving me a ride home again. He said so in the note he left in our birdhouse the other day."

"You're sure the lucky one." Susie sighed. "Wish I had the promise of a ride home with some cute fellow tonight."

Melinda patted Susie's hand. "Your time will come. Just wait and see."

"Jah, well, I'm twenty years old already. Many Amish women my age are married by now. I'll probably end up to be *en alt maedel.* Could be I'll spend the rest of my days workin' at Kaulp's General Store and never have a husband or family of my own."

"Oh, you won't either be an old maid. I doubt you'll be workin' for Kaulp's the rest of your life, either. One of these days you'll—"

Susie jumped up, jostling Melinda and nearly tossing her out of the swing. "Let's not talk about this anymore. Some buggies have pulled into the driveway, and one of them belongs to Bishop Frey. Church will be starting soon, so we'd better get inside."

"You go on," Melinda said. "I'm gonna sit here awhile. Once we're all in the house, it will be hot and stuffy."

"Okay." Susie went in the front door, and Melinda resumed her swinging.

A few minutes later, John Frey and his wife, Margaret, stepped onto the porch. The bishop walked with a limp these days and was beginning to show his age, but he could still preach God's Word and lead the people. Melinda figured he would continue as bishop for several more years before he died.

"Gude mariye," Margaret said, as they approached Melinda.

" 'Mornin'," she answered with a nod.

"You plannin' to be baptized and join the church soon?" the bishop asked.

Melinda could hardly believe the man had posed such a question. Was Bishop John's memory failing him the way Grandpa Hertzler's seemed to be? It was a shame to witness older folks forgetting so many things.

"I got baptized last year, Bishop John. It was soon after my eighteenth birthday," she said.

The wrinkles in the bishop's forehead deepened, and he gave his long gray beard a couple of sharp pulls. Then he narrowed his eyes and stared at Melinda so hard she began to squirm. "Hmm . . . Well, jah, that's right, you were one of those I baptized last year."

Maybe the man's memory isn't going after all. Might could be his problem is just failing eyesight. Melinda had felt bad when her mother began to lose her close-up vision and started wearing reading glasses, but Mama had laughed and said, "That's what comes with getting older."

Melinda was glad she had several more years until she had to face getting old, and so far her vision had been good, too. Of course, she knew a couple of young Amish women who had worn glasses ever since they were in school, so poor eyesight wasn't necessarily an age-related thing.

Margaret smiled and adjusted her own metal-framed glasses, which had slipped to the end of her nose. Then she leaned over and patted her husband's arm. "Shall we go inside now, John? The service will be starting soon."

The bishop released a noisy yawn. "Jah, guess we'd better."

As soon as John and Margaret stepped into the house, Melinda left the swing and headed for the barn.

Think I'll go see how much the kittens Susie's cat gave birth to a few weeks ago have grown.

For the next several minutes, Melinda sat on a bale of straw watching Daisy feed her six squirming babies. *All baby animals are cute. Some more than others.*

Sometime later, Melinda left the barn, and as soon as she closed the door, she realized that preaching service had already begun. The chant-like voices of the people singing inside her grandparents' house filtered through the open windows. She hurriedly entered through the back door and tiptoed down the hall. Backless wooden benches filled the large living room and spilled over into the parlor. The rooms were separated by a removable wall that was taken out whenever preaching services were held in this home.

As Melinda slipped quietly into the main room, a few people looked up from their hymnbooks and glanced her way. Most, however, stayed focused on the song they were singing.

Susie was one who noticed Melinda, and she motioned her over to the bench where she was sitting. There was an empty spot on the end, and Melinda figured her aunt had been saving it for her.

"Where have you been?" Susie whispered when Melinda sat down.

"Out in the barn with Daisy and her brood. They're sure cute."

Susie didn't say anything, just slowly shook her head. *She doesn't understand Sometimes I wonder how*

Susie and I can be such good friends when we don't think alike on the subject of animals.

She glanced across the room at the men and boys who were seated opposite them. Gabe sat beside his friend Aaron, and she caught him staring at her. He'd probably seen her sneak into the room, and she wondered if he thought she was irresponsible for being late. Would he say something about it later on?

Gabe's friendly smile and quick wink caused Melinda's heart to flutter. It was enough to let her know he wasn't judging her.

She shivered at the anticipation of spending time with him tonight at the singing and afterward when he drove her home in his buggy.

Melinda's thoughts spun faster than a windmill in a gale. Maybe this would be the night of their first kiss. And maybe, if she could think of the right way to say it, Melinda would open her heart and tell Gabe what Dr. Franklin had suggested she do.

A nudge to the ribs brought Melinda's thoughts to a halt. "You're not paying attention," Susie hissed.

"I am so."

Susie leaned closer and whispered in Melinda's ear, "You're paying attention to Gabe, but that's about all."

Melinda sat up straight and folded her hands. If her aunt had noticed her preoccupation with Gabe, others might have as well. She was thankful her mother sat three rows ahead. Hopefully Mama hadn't noticed Melinda's late arrival, for if she had, Melinda would probably be in for a lecture after church.

Melinda turned her attention to the front of the room, where Preacher Kaulp had begun the first sermon of the day. He spoke from the book of Proverbs on the subject of wisdom.

Wisdom is what I need. Wisdom to know if I should separate myself from those I love in order to become a vet so I can properly care for sick and injured animals.

She closed her eyes. *Lord, You know that Mama and Papa Noah already think I spend too much time with my animal friends, and if they knew what I was contemplating it would break their hearts. Please give me the wisdom to know what to do, and if leaving the Amish faith is right for me, then give me a sense of peace and help those I love to understand.*

Gabe was glad when the church service was over. Not that he hadn't enjoyed the sermons or time of singing, for he had listened intently to the scripture verse Bishop Frey quoted near the end of his lengthy sermon. It was from Proverbs 18:22: "Whoso findeth a wife findeth a good thing, and obtaineth favour of the Lord."

Those words from the Bible made Gabe even more determined to make Melinda his wife. In fact, if everything went well tonight, he might even get up the nerve to propose. If Melinda accepted, he hoped they could be married sometime this fall. And at the very least, he planned to kiss her before she left his buggy and went into her house.

From Gabe's vantage point under the shade of a walnut tree, he saw Melinda on the front porch talking to her aunts Grace and Esther.

I wonder if they're chewin' her out for being late to church this morning. He'd seen them turn around when Melinda entered the room.

Gabe flopped onto the grass and leaned against the trunk of the tree. He had just closed his eyes when he heard female voices nearby.

His eyes popped open, and he glanced to the left. Barbara Hilty and Melinda's mother, Faith, were heading his way.

"I wish I knew what to do about Melinda," Faith said. "She was late to church this morning, and when I questioned her about it, she said she'd gone out to the barn and lost track of time."

Gabe's ears perked up. He wasn't trying to eavesdrop, but he was curious to hear what else Melinda's mamm might have to say.

"Sometimes raising teenagers can be just as hard as when they were kinner," Barbara Hilty said. "Guess we'll be trying to steer them in the right direction until they get married and leave home."

"Jah," Faith agreed. "I have a feeling that time isn't too far off for Melinda, either. She's been seeing Gabe Swartz, but I believe she thinks we're in the dark about it."

Barbara chuckled. "My Aaron claims he's never gettin' married. Maybe he plans to stick around home and be told what to do for the rest of his life."

The two women strolled past the cluster of trees where Gabe sat. He quickly pulled his straw hat down over his eyes, plucked up a blade of grass, and stuck it between his teeth, hoping to look inconspicuous. Faith and Barbara continued on their way, apparently unaware of his presence.

He drew in a deep breath and said a prayer for himself and Melinda. *Someday, Lord willing, we'll have our own kinner to worry about.*

five

"It's nice of you to want to drive us to the singing, but I don't see why we couldn't have walked to the Hiltys' place. It isn't that far," Melinda said to Grandpa Stutzman as she settled herself on the buggy seat between him and Susie.

"I won't have my youngest daughter or my grand-daughter out walkin' in the dark no matter how close we are to the Hiltys'."

Melinda glanced over at her aunt to gauge her reaction, but Susie only shrugged.

"I'll be back to pick you up around ten," Grandpa said.

"Oh, Melinda won't be needin' a ride," Susie blurted out. "She's already been promised one from—"

Melinda poked Susie on the arm. "Hush."

"Uh—what I meant to say was, I'll be the only one needing a ride home from the singing."

"How do you know some young fellow won't be

askin' to bring you home?" Grandpa's bushy gray eyebrows lifted into his hairline. "Huh?"

Susie stared at her hands clasped in her lap. "Don't know who it would be."

Melinda's heart went out to her aunt. It wasn't right that a woman Susie's age didn't have a steady boyfriend.

"How about I come by a little later?" Grandpa said, smiling at his daughter. "That way you'll be sure to have a way home in case all the young men are too shy to ask."

Susie gave a quick nod. "Guess that would be all right."

As much as Melinda wanted to spend time alone with Gabe, she couldn't stand the thought of Susie being picked up by her daed. It was bad enough he'd insisted on driving them to the singing. "If Susie doesn't get asked, Gabe and I will bring her home."

Grandpa chuckled. "Gabe, is it? I might have known."

Melinda covered her mouth with the palm of her hand. "I—I meant to say, Susie can ride with me and my date."

"I know," Grandpa said with a grin. "And if Susie's okay with that, it's fine by me."

Susie shook her head. "I don't think it's a good idea."

"Why not?" Melinda looked over at Susie, wondering what she could be thinking.

"I'm not going to be a fifth wheel on the buggy."

Susie leaned close to Melinda's ear. "What if Gabe wants to kiss you tonight?"

Melinda's heart beat a little faster. She'd been looking forward to Gabe taking her home and hopefully offering that first kiss. "It'll be fine," she said. "We'll drop you off first, then Gabe can take me home."

Susie nodded. "Jah, okay."

A short while later, they pulled into the Hiltys' driveway. Grandpa drove past the house, and then the harness shop, stopping the buggy near the barn. "Here ya go. Hope you both have yourselves a real *gut* time."

"Thanks, Papa." Susie hopped out of the buggy and sprinted toward the barn, where peals of laughter and chattering voices drifted on the night air.

Melinda turned to face her grandfather. "She'll be fine, Grandpa. You'll see."

"I know, but it sure would be nice if she found herself a beau." He picked up the reins. "Now go have some fun, and be sure to tell Gabe Swartz I said he's gettin' one fine girl."

Melinda's face warmed, and she leaned over to kiss her grandfather's wrinkled cheek. "I love you, Grandpa."

"That goes double for me."

She patted his arm, then climbed out of the buggy. "See you soon."

"Yep." Grandpa backed the horse up and headed down the driveway.

As Melinda hurried to the barn, the rhythm of her heartbeat kept time with her footsteps. She could hardly wait to see Gabe.

Gabe stood at the refreshment table, about to ladle some punch into a paper cup for Melinda, whom he'd spotted on the other side of the barn.

"Gettin' some sweets for your sweetie?" Aaron teased as he stepped up beside Gabe.

"What do you think?"

"I think you'd get down on your hands and knees and lap water like a dog if Melinda asked you to."

Gabe grunted and rubbed the side of his nose. "Would not. Besides, she's already got plenty of pets."

"Jah, well, she might want one more."

Gabe turned to face his friend. "Are you tryin' to goad me into an argument this evening?"

Aaron chuckled. "Who me? Never!"

"Yeah, right." Gabe grabbed two peanut butter cookies, a handful of pretzels, and a wedge of cheese, then piled them on a paper plate.

"Are you takin' Melinda home tonight after the singing?"

"What do you think?"

"You sure do like to answer my questions with a question of your own." Aaron bumped Gabe's arm, nearly knocking the plate out of his hands.

"Hey, watch it!"

"Sorry."

"You plannin' to offer anyone a ride home?" Gabe

asked, hoping the change of subject might get Aaron out of his teasing mode.

"No way! I'm not ready to get tied down yet."

"Who said anything about getting tied down? You can take a girl home without proposing marriage, ya know." Gabe wasn't about to tell his friend that a marriage proposal was in his plans for the night. Aaron would only taunt him that much more.

Aaron snatched one of Gabe's cookies and bit into it. "Yeah, but as soon as you give some female a ride in your buggy, then she starts thinkin' you want to court her. After that, the next thing on her mind is marriage." He shook his head. "I ain't ready for that. All's I want right now is to own my daed's business."

Gabe lifted his eyebrows. "Paul's plannin' to quit workin' at the harness shop?"

"Not yet, but someday he'll be ready to retire. When that time comes, I'm gonna be ready. My real daed wanted me to have the shop he started, ya know."

Gabe nodded. "I'm sure Paul does, too."

"Maybe so."

Gabe moved away from the table, and Aaron followed. "To tell ya the truth, I think my daed still sees me as a little kid who doesn't know nearly as much as him about makin' things. As you know, I'm the youngest in the family, with four sisters who are all married and out on their own."

"What's that got to do with anything?" Aaron asked.

"Ever since I was little, Pap, Mom, and even my sisters have treated me like a *boppli*. I believe my daed likes being in charge of everything and telling me what to do all the time."

"I'm not really treated like a baby, but my stepdad sure likes to order me around."

"Guess in the eyes of our parents we'll never be grown up," Gabe said with a frown.

"You're probably right." Aaron bit off the end of one fingernail and spit it on the straw-covered floor.

Gabe wrinkled his nose. "That was so nasty. Where are your manners, anyhow?"

Aaron lowered his gaze and looked kind of sheepish. "Sorry. Nail bitin's a bad habit that I probably should break. Least that's what my mamm thinks."

"So why don't ya quit?"

"Maybe I will some day . . . when I have a good enough reason to."

"Well, Melinda's waitin' for me, so I'd better get over there with this food," Gabe said, deciding it was time to move on.

Aaron patted Gabe on the back. "You do that, you lovesick *hundel*."

Gabe shrugged his friend's hand away. "I ain't no love-sick pup."

"Okay then, you're a lovesick man."

Gabe swallowed a retort and headed across the room. He knew Aaron was only funning with him, and if the tables were turned, he'd probably do the same. Right now he had other things on his mind.

For the next couple of hours, Gabe sat beside

Melinda and enjoyed singing, visiting, and eating with the other young people who had come to the singing.

Shortly before things wound down, Melinda was called on to lead the group in some yodeling. Her face turned red, but after some coaxing from Gabe and a few other friends, she finally agreed. While several others in attendance could yodel fairly well, nobody did it as expertly as Melinda.

Maybe that's because her mother used to be a professional yodeler, Gabe thought as he sat on a bale of straw and watched Melinda. Her hands were cupped around her mouth, and she grinned from ear to ear as she belted out, "Oddle-lay—oddle-lay—oddle-lay dee-tee. My mama was an old cowhand, and she taught me how to yodel before I could stand—yo—le—tee—yo—le—tee—hi ho!"

Gabe glanced around the room and saw that all eyes were trained on his girlfriend. He figured he was the luckiest man here, and the other fellows must surely be envious.

As Melinda sat beside Gabe in his open buggy, she closed her eyes and breathed in the sweet perfume given off by the trees and flowers that were bursting with spring buds. The temperature was just right this evening, and she'd noticed earlier that a full moon had cast a ray of light on the road ahead.

"You sleepin'?" Gabe asked.

She opened her eyes and smiled at him. "Just enjoying the fresh air and peaceful ride."

"It is a nice evening." He draped his arm across her shoulders, bringing them so dose she could smell the pine-scented soap he must have used when he'd gotten ready for the singing tonight. "You warm enough?"

"I'm fine."

They rode in silence for a while, with the only sounds being the steady *clip-clop* of the horse's hooves and an occasional hoot of an owl. Melinda thought about the singing and how Susie hung around some of the other young women her age most of the evening, while Gabe stuck close to Melinda much of the time. Poor Susie never did pair off with any of the young men in attendance. Even during the time of yodeling Melinda had led and the singing of lively songs like "Mocking Bird Hill" and "Yellow Rose of Texas," Susie appeared glum. "I Never Will Marry" seemed more like her song. Aaron's, too, for that matter.

When it came time for them to leave, Susie informed Melinda that she'd found a ride home with Kathy and Rebecca Yoder, so she wouldn't have to tag along with Melinda and Gabe. Melinda didn't argue, knowing once Susie made up her mind about something, she wasn't likely to budge. Besides, Melinda really did want to be alone with Gabe during the whole ride home.

"Say, Gabe, I was wondering if you might have the time to build me a couple more cages for my animals," she asked suddenly.

"Hmm . . . I'd like to, Melinda, but right now me and Pap are really busy in the shop." He smiled. "I will try to squeeze it into whatever free time I have, though."

"*Danki.* I'd appreciate that."

"Do you ever think about your real daed or find yourself wishing you and your mamm had stayed in the English world?" Gabe's unexpected question startled Melinda, and she sat up straight. Did he have an inkling of what she was thinking about doing? Had Gabe seen Dr. Franklin recently, and could the man have mentioned his recent suggestion that Melinda think about becoming a vet?

"What would make you ask me such a question?" she asked, looking at Gabe out of the corner of her eye.

"If there's even a chance you might want to return to the English way of life, I feel I have the right to know."

Melinda drew in a quick breath. Since Gabe had brought up the subject, maybe now was the time to discuss Dr. Franklin's idea. She squeezed her eyes shut, searching for just the right words, and when she opened them again, she was shocked to see a man standing in the middle of the road not far ahead. He had his back to them, but she could tell by his dark clothes and hat that he was Amish. "Gabe, look out!" she hollered.

He pulled sharply on the reins. "Whoa there! Steady boy."

When the horse stopped, Gabe grabbed a flashlight

from under the seat, and he and Melinda jumped down from the buggy.

The man in the road turned around, and Melinda's mouth fell open. "Grandpa Hertzler?"

Her grandfather didn't answer. He just stood there staring at Melinda as though she were a complete stranger.

"He looks confused, like he doesn't know where he is," Gabe whispered.

Melinda nodded. "We've got to get him home."

"Levi, it's Gabe and Melinda," Gabe said, gently taking hold of Grandpa's arm.

Grandpa studied him a few seconds, then turned to face Melinda. Finally, a look of recognition crossed his face. "What are you doin' out here, girl?"

"Gabe was giving me a ride home from the singing. We stopped the buggy when we saw you in the middle of the road." She grabbed his other arm. "Don't you know how dangerous it is to be out walking after dark? Especially dressed in clothes that aren't bright."

The confusion she saw on her grandfather's face made Melinda's heart ache. He'd obviously wandered off their property and onto the road. She was sure Mama and Papa Noah had no idea where he was.

"Let's get into the buggy, and I'll drive you both home," Gabe said.

Melinda was relieved when her grandfather went willingly, but she could see by the frown on Gabe's face that he wasn't happy when Grandpa took a seat next to him, which left Melinda sitting on the outside edge.

50

She reached for Grandpa's hand and gave it a gentle squeeze. The buggy ride might not have been the romantic one she had hoped for, but at least Grandpa was safe. Maybe she and Gabe would have another chance to be alone soon. And maybe by then she would be better prepared to discuss her future with him.

six

"Good morning, Melinda," Dr. Franklin said when she stepped into the veterinary clinic on a Monday morning a few weeks after the singing. "How are you this fine sunny day?"

"I'm fine. How are things here?"

The middle-aged man's blue eyes twinkled, and he wiggled his eyebrows. "Got a squirrel in this morning with an injured foot."

Melinda moved quickly to the counter where he stood. "How bad is it hurt? Will it be okay? What are you planning to do with it once you've doctored its foot?"

The doctor laughed and held up his hand. "One question at a time, please."

"Sorry. I do tend to be eager when it comes to suffering animals."

"I know you do. Now to answer your first question: the wound isn't deep, and I think the squirrel might have had its foot stepped on."

She frowned. "Who would do something that mean?"

"Probably wasn't done on purpose." He reached up to scratch the side of his head, where streaks of gray showed through his closely cropped brown hair. "Tommy Curtis brought the critter in, saying he'd found it lying beside a maple tree near his school."

"Will you keep the squirrel here until it's better?" she asked.

He grinned. "Thought maybe you'd like to take it home until it's ready to be set free, which should only be a few days from now, I'm guessing."

Melinda nodded eagerly. "I don't have many spare cages right now, but I did find an old one at a yard sale awhile back. Guess I could keep him in that until his foot's healed."

"I'll give you some ointment to put on the wound, and you can take the squirrel home with you this evening."

Melinda smiled as she donned her work apron. It felt good to know the doctor trusted her enough to care for the squirrel. Of course, if the animal's injuries were serious, she was sure he would keep it at the clinic. "Guess I'd better get busy with the cleaning," she said, moving toward the door where the animal cages were kept.

"Before you get started, I'd like to ask you a question," Dr. Franklin said, stepping around the front of the counter.

"What is it?"

"I'm wondering if you've had a chance to think over the things we talked about a few weeks ago or have looked at the brochures I gave you on the school of veterinary medicine I attended in New Jersey."

"I did read through the information, and I've been thinking and praying about it." Melinda pursed her lips. "I think I'd like to become a veterinarian, but it would mean getting a college education, and that goes against our Amish beliefs."

The doctor's dark eyebrows drew together. "I've lived in Seymour for several years and know most of the Amish in the area. Yet I still don't understand all their rules and regulations."

"We believe the Bible instructs us to be separate from the world," she explained. "We're not against education and learning from others, but progressive education could lead to worldliness."

He took a step toward her. "So you're saying you've decided not to pursue a career in veterinary medicine?"

"No, that's not what I'm sayin'. There's so much to be considered, and I haven't been able to think it all through. I haven't said anything to my folks yet, either."

"I understand. It is a big decision, so take your time, Melinda."

She nodded. "When I do finally decide, I'll be sure and let you know."

Gabe grabbed a stack of sandpaper as he started working on the tops of some kitchen cabinets one of their English neighbors had ordered a few weeks earlier. He hoped the week would go by quickly because he was anxious for Saturday to get here. He and his folks had been invited to Melinda's birthday party, and he looked forward to presenting her with the little fawn he'd carved. It had turned out well, and he was glad Noah would be giving Melinda the birdhouse instead of him. Noah had stopped by on his way to the Christmas tree farm this morning to pick it up. Gabe was pleased when he'd complimented him on a job well done. He just hoped Melinda would like the wooden deer. To make it useful and not purely decorative, he'd glued the little critter to a small chunk of wood and planned to suggest she use it as a doorstop.

Sure hope I'll be able to spend a few minutes alone with her on Saturday night, Gabe thought. *Haven't been able to be off by ourselves since I took her home from the singing a few weeks ago and we found her grandpa standing in the road.* At the rate things were going, Gabe wondered if he'd ever get the chance to kiss Melinda, much less ask her to marry him.

"From the way you're swipin' that sandpaper across the cabinet tops, there might not be anything left. I'd say your thoughts must be on something other than work this morning," Pap said, stepping up beside Gabe.

"Guess I was thinkin' about Saturday night."

"Looking forward to Melinda's birthday party, I imagine." Pap's blue eyes twinkled when he grinned at Gabe.

"Jah."

"It was nice of her folks to include your mamm and me in the invitation."

"We've known their family a long time, so I guess it's only natural that they'd want all three of us to be there."

"Probably would have asked your sisters to come if they were still livin' at home," Pap added.

Gabe nodded, wondering if his daed knew he and Melinda were courting. He hadn't told his folks that he was seeing her or that he planned to ask her to marry him, but Gabe knew Pap was no dummy and could have put two and two together by now.

"Sure hope this nice weather holds out and we can have the party outside," he said.

Pap raked his fingers through his full brown beard, which was generously peppered with gray. "Yep. It's been a nice few weeks of May so far. Makes me wish I had some free time to go fishin'." He turned toward the rear of the shop with a shrug. "Guess I'd best get back to work on that rocking chair Abe Yutzy ordered last week."

"Holler if you need any help."

"Danki, but I think I can manage. You'd best stick with the project you're workin' on now."

"Say, Pap."

"What is it, Gabe?"

"You think we might broaden the business to include more than just cabinets and basic furniture? I'd sure like the chance to work on some other things."

"Naw, I don't think so. We've got our hands full just makin' what we do now."

Gabe gritted his teeth as his father walked away.

55

Will he ever see me as capable? He grabbed a fresh piece of sandpaper and gave the top of the cabinet a few good swipes. *As soon as I get enough money saved up, I'm going to open my own woodworking business, and I plan to make a lot more things than just cabinets and a few basic pieces of furniture.*

When Melinda arrived home that evening with the squirrel she had named Cinnamon, she headed straight for the barn. She set the cardboard box with the squirrel inside on a small wooden table and reached for a pair of leather gloves hanging on a nail. It wouldn't be a good idea to handle the critter with her bare hands. It wasn't tame like Reba seemed to be, and she didn't want to risk getting bitten.

Melinda located the spare cage and reached inside the box to retrieve Cinnamon.

He didn't squirm or try to get away, and she figured it was probably because of his hurt foot. When she closed the door on the cage, she discovered that the latch was broken and wouldn't stay shut.

"I don't need you getting out, Cinnamon," Melinda muttered. "At least not until your foot is healed." She headed across the barn in search of some wire, but before she could locate it, Papa Noah stepped into the building.

"Guder owed," he said with a smile. "How was your day?"

"Good evening to you, too," Melinda replied. "My day was fine until now."

"What's the trouble?"

Melinda pointed to the cage with Cinnamon inside. "The latch on the cage door is broken, and I was looking for some wire to hold it shut."

Papa Noah moved over to the cage. "Where'd ya get the squirrel, and what happened to its foot?"

"Got him from Dr. Franklin. Some English boy in Seymour found him outside the schoolhouse, and the poor critter had a cut on his foot."

"So why isn't the vet takin' care of him, instead of you?"

"The doctor did all he could, but he didn't want to turn Cinnamon loose until the wound had healed." Melinda grinned. "So he gave him to me for safe-keeping."

Papa Noah shook his head. "If you're not careful, you're gonna have so many critters around here that they'll be takin' over the place." He motioned to the cage. "Guess if you keep him in here it will be all right, but we'll have to wire that door shut."

"That's what I was about to do, but I haven't been able to find any wire."

"I know right where it is." Papa Noah headed across the barn and opened up a toolbox sitting on a shelf.

A short time later, he had the cage door wired shut. "I didn't make it too tight, because I know you'll need to get inside to give the squirrel food and water," he said.

She nodded. "Danki. I appreciate the help."

"Should we head for the house and see what your

mamm's got for supper?" he asked, nodding toward the barn door.

"You go ahead. I want to check on Reba the raccoon and the baby goat before I come in."

He shrugged. "Jah, okay, but don't be too long. I'm sure your mamm could use your help in the kitchen, and you know how she gets when you spend too much time takin' care of your critters."

Melinda knew all too well how Mama felt about her animal friends. She'd never seemed to mind a couple of pets hanging around, but when Melinda started bringing home creatures that lived in the woods, her mother was less understanding.

"I won't be but a few minutes," she promised.

"Okay. See you at supper then." Papa Noah lifted his hand in a wave and went out the door.

seven

Melinda couldn't remember when she'd been so excited about one of her birthdays.

"I wonder what Gabe will give me," she murmured as she stepped into a blue cotton dress in preparation for the big event. "I'm sure it'll be something he's made. Gabe is so talented, he can take any piece of wood and turn it into something beautiful."

The twittering of birds outside Melinda's open window drew her attention outdoors. At least she knew that Cinnamon, the squirrel Dr. Franklin had put in her care, wasn't chasing any of the birds. This

58

morning she'd let the critter out of his cage for a bit and later caught him trying to eat at one of the bird-feeders. After that, she'd put him back in the cage, and he would stay there until his foot was healed and she could set him free in the woods.

A warm breeze coming through her bedroom window made the dark curtains dance. Melinda drew in a deep breath and headed downstairs, excited that her guests would be arriving soon.

Outside, she discovered Papa Noah lighting the barbecue. He'd set up two large tables with benches, and Mama had covered them with green plastic tablecloths.

"It looks like we're about ready," Melinda remarked to her stepfather.

"Now all we need is our guests," he said with a chuckle.

"They'll be here soon, I expect." She took a seat on the end of the bench closest to the barbecue grill. "Where's Grandpa Hertzler? I thought he'd be out here already."

Papa Noah blew out his breath. "I'm not sure what to do about him."

"You mean his forgetfulness?"

"Jah. I reminded my daed this morning about your birthday party, but when I went over to his side of the house a few minutes ago, I found him asleep in his favorite chair."

"Maybe he's just tired."

"I thought that at first, but then I woke him up and

59

suggested he get ready for the party, and he gave me a bewildered look. He didn't seem to have any idea what I was talking about."

Melinda frowned. "It's hard to understand why some days he seems pretty good and other days he barely knows who we are."

"Your mamm made him a doctor's appointment in Springfield. I'm hoping they'll run some tests that will help us know what's wrong."

"Sounds like a good idea."

"I hear a buggy rumblin' up the driveway," Papa Noah said, glancing to the left. "Why don't ya go see who's the first to arrive?"

Melinda stood. "Jah, okay."

When she rounded the corner of the house, she was greeted by Gabe and his parents, Stephen and Leah Swartz.

Gabe offered her a friendly smile. "Happy birthday, Melinda."

"Happy birthday," Gabe's folks said in unison.

"Danki." Melinda nodded toward the house. "Papa Noah has the barbecue fired up, and Mama's in the kitchen. So feel free to go out back or inside, whichever you like."

"I believe I'll go in the house and see if there's anything I can do to help Faith," Leah said.

"And I'll head around back and find out what Noah's up to," Stephen put in.

As soon as his folks left, Gabe stepped up beside Melinda. "You sure look pretty tonight."

She felt heat radiate up the back of her neck and spread quickly to her cheeks. "I don't think I look much different than the last time you saw me."

He leaned in closer, until she could feel his warm breath tickle her ear. "You're the prettiest woman I know."

"Danki."

"You want to open my gift now or wait until later?" he asked, lifting the paper sack he held in one hand.

"I guess it would be best to wait and open all my gifts at the same time."

"Jah, okay." Gabe smiled as he studied her intently, and she felt her toes curl inside her black leather shoes.

"Hey, Gabe! What are you up to?"

Melinda whirled around to face her brother. "Isaiah, you shouldn't sneak up on people like that."

"Wasn't sneakin'. Just happened to come around the house in time to see the two of you makin' eyes at each other."

Gabe ruffled Isaiah's hair. "You're right—we're caught."

"Why don't you go see if Papa Noah needs any help?" Melinda suggested.

Isaiah squinted. "I've never figured out why you call him that. Can't ya just say, 'Papa,' without addin' the Noah part?"

"I was seven years old when Mama married Papa Noah. He's been like a daed to me all these years, but he's not my real father. So I've always thought it best to call him Papa Noah, and he's never complained or asked me to call him anything else."

Isaiah shrugged. "Guess I'll mosey around back and see what's cookin'."

"We'll be there soon," Melinda called to his retreating form. Gabe reached for Melinda's hand and drew her aside. "As I was sayin' before Isaiah came along—"

Two more buggies rolled into the yard just then, and Gabe released a moan. "Guess what I wanted to say will have to wait 'til later." He gave Melinda's hand a gentle squeeze. "Maybe after the party winds down, we can take a walk."

She nodded. "I'd like that."

Melinda bit into a piece of moist chocolate cake and savored the moment. Her family and closest friends were here—Gabe and his folks, Grandpa and Grandma Stutzman with Susie, Barbara and Paul Hilty with their six children, and her immediate family—Mama, Papa Noah, Isaiah, and Grandpa Hertzler. She had received plenty of gifts, and each one was special. The best gift of all was the little fawn Gabe had whittled and glued to a small log. He'd said it would make a good doorstop, and she had to agree. She saw Gabe's present as an affirmation that he too liked animals. Maybe before the evening was out she would know just how much.

The birdhouse from Papa Noah, which he said Gabe had also made, was another favorite gift. Melinda had been pleased to discover the separate compartment Gabe had added so they could keep sending notes to each other and not have to worry about the birds making a nest on top of their messages.

Another special present was from Susie, who had given Melinda one of Daisy's sweet little kittens. It was a female with pure white fur, and Melinda decided to call it Snow. Since her mother had commented that the kitten would make a nice pet, Melinda figured it would be allowed in the house.

Melinda was just finishing her piece of cake when the wind became restless and clouds raced overhead. Minutes later, it started to rain. Everyone grabbed something off the table and dashed for the house. *There goes my walk with Gabe. It doesn't look like we'll get any time alone tonight.*

"Whew! What a downpour," Mama said as they entered the kitchen. "It amazes me how swiftly the weather can change during the spring."

Melinda placed her kitten on the floor, and Snow scurried under the stove. The older guests found seats around the kitchen table, while the younger ones—Isaiah and Barbara's children, Joseph, Zachary, David, Emma, and Bessie—went to the living room to play games. Melinda, Gabe, Susie, and Aaron, headed outside to watch the storm from the safety of the front porch. Melinda wished it could have been just her and Gabe, but she knew it wouldn't be polite to exclude her other guests.

"I sure like watching the way *wedderleech* zigzags

across the sky," Gabe commented with a sweep of his hand.

"I've always been afraid of the *dunner,*" Susie put in.

"It ain't the thunder that can hurt you," Aaron asserted. "It's those bolts of dangerous lightning you've got to worry about."

Melinda shivered and rubbed her hands over her arms.

"You cold?" Gabe asked.

"A little. I should have grabbed a sweater before comin' outside."

"What was that?"

She raised her voice to be heard over the thud of more thunder. "Jah, I'm a little bit cold."

"Does this help?" Gabe stood behind Melinda and wrapped his arms around her waist.

"It does." She closed her eyes and leaned into him, as her breathing quickened. "Sure hope all my critters are doin' okay. Most animals don't like storms."

"At least we know Snow's all right," Susie put in. "She's probably curled up in someone's lap by now."

Aaron turned around. "I'm tired of watchin' the rain. Think I'll head back inside and see what the kinner are doin'."

Susie nodded. "Maybe I should, too."

Melinda smiled. She figured their friends were trying to give her and Gabe some time alone. Gabe must have known also, for he squeezed her a bit tighter.

As soon as Aaron and Susie entered the house, Gabe led Melinda over to the porch swing. Once they were seated, he draped his arm across her shoulders and pulled her close to his side. "Happy birthday, beautiful Melinda."

She opened her mouth to respond, but before she could get a word out, he lowered his head and brushed her lips with his.

Melinda melted into his embrace and wrapped her hands around his neck. Their first kiss was even better than she had expected.

Suddenly the front door flew open, and Isaiah stuck his head out. "Oh, yuk! I'll never kiss any girl 'cept Mama."

Melinda's cheeks burned hot as she shook her finger. "You say one word about what you saw here, and I'll tell Papa Noah that your dog ate out of a pie pan the other day."

"Aw, Jericho wasn't hurtin' nothin'." Isaiah stuck out his tongue. "Besides, the plate got washed."

Melinda jumped up, ready to tell her little brother what she thought of his juvenile antics, but a flash of fur darted over her foot, raced across the porch, and dove inside the open doorway.

"Cinnamon!" she shouted. "How did you get out of your cage?"

eight

Melinda dashed into the house after the runaway squirrel, and Gabe followed right on her heels. He couldn't believe the way things were going tonight.

First, the rain had put a damper on their plans to take a walk. Then Melinda's younger brother had interrupted them when he was on the verge of proposing. Now a silly critter had come along and ruined things.

Pandemonium broke out as soon as they entered the living room. Not only was the squirrel skittering all over the place, but Melinda's new kitten seemed to be the squirrel's prey. The two animals circled the room, darting under chairs, banging into walls, and sliding across the hardwood floor. When Snow crawled under the braided oval throw rug, Cinnamon pounced on her. The kitten sailed out and zipped to the other side of the room.

"You get the cat, and I'll corner the squirrel," Gabe shouted to Melinda.

Aaron, Susie, and the children, who'd been playing games in the adjoining room, came on the scene and became part of the chase, but no one had any luck catching either animal.

"Have you got any paper sacks?" Gabe called to Isaiah.

"I think there's some in the kitchen."

"Get four of the biggest ones you can find!"

When Isaiah returned a few minutes later, the older folks were with him.

"What's going on here?" Noah asked with a look of concern. "Isaiah said something about a squirrel."

"Cinnamon got out of his cage somehow and ended up in the house," Melinda panted. "Now he's after Snow."

"The squirrel's gonna eat the cat," five-year-old

Emma hollered. When Cinnamon whizzed past the child, she jumped and squealed, then ran for cover behind her mother's long green dress.

"Settle down," Barbara said, taking hold of Emma's hand. "Let's go to the kitchen and let the others handle this."

"She needs our help."

"We're gonna trap 'em."

"They're just a couple of desperate critters."

"Come here, Snow."

"Easy, Cinnamon."

Everyone spoke at once, and the animals kept circling the living room. Finally, Noah held up his hands. "Everybody, please calm down." He turned to Isaiah. "What are the paper sacks for?"

The boy shrugged. "I don't know. Gabe asked me to get 'em."

Gabe grinned, and with a self-conscious swipe of his nose, he said, "Thought if the four of us each took a sack, we might be able to trap Cinnamon or Snow inside one of the bags."

"I believe I have a better plan." Noah turned back to Isaiah. "Please go to the kitchen and get a broom from the utility closet."

Melinda's eyes were huge as silver dollars as she grasped her stepfather's arm. "I hope you're not going to smack either one of my pets."

Faith spoke up. "Only one of them is a pet, Melinda, and I'm sure your daed wouldn't intentionally hurt either animal."

Grandpa Hertzler sank into the closest chair. "Put the broom away. I hate housework. Always did." He shook his head, and his white beard moved back and forth across his chest like the pendulum on the clock above the fireplace.

"We're not going to clean house, Pop," Noah said. "And I don't plan to do the animals any harm. Now hurry and get me that broom, Isaiah."

The boy shoved the paper sacks at Gabe and scurried out of the room.

Gabe handed one sack to Melinda, one to Aaron and Susie, and kept the other one for himself. He crouched down and opened his sack, telling the others to do the same. "If either the cat or the squirrel comes your way, try to scoop it into the bag."

Noah shook his head. "I don't think that's going to work. I believe my way's better." He cupped his hands around his mouth. "Isaiah, where is that broom?"

"I'll go," Melinda's mother offered.

Just then Isaiah dashed into the room, flung the broom at his father, and scuttled off to one side with an expectant look on his face.

"Somebody, open the front door!"

Melinda rushed to do as her stepfather commanded.

Gabe groaned. Whatever Noah had in mind, he was sure it would fail. He remained on his knees, waiting patiently for either the squirrel or the kitten to pass his way again. A few seconds later, Cinnamon skittered across the floor in front of Gabe's paper sack, and Noah's broom swooshed past the critter's bushy tail.

Cinnamon took off like a flash of lightning and zipped out the open door.

The cat darted under the sofa, and no amount of coaxing on Melinda or Susie's part could bring her out.

"Just leave her be," Noah said as he headed for the kitchen with the other adults.

"That's right. She'll come out when she's good and ready," Paul Hilty called over his shoulder.

As Gabe stood, his heart went out to Melinda. She looked so dejected. What had started out to be such a nice birthday party had quickly turned into complete mayhem.

"Come on, the excitement's over. Let's head back to the dining room and finish those games we started," Aaron said to the others.

The children and teens followed him out of the room, but Melinda stayed in a kneeling position and continued to call her kitten. "Here, Snow," she pleaded. "You can come out now because the squirrel's gone."

Gabe shifted from one foot to the other, unsure of what to do. He thought about offering to go outside and look for the squirrel, but that would be ridiculous. It was still raining, and Cinnamon was probably halfway to Seymour by now.

For lack of anything better to do, he flopped into a chair and sat there with his arms folded, staring out the window at the pouring rain and streaks of lightning.

• • •

"Come, Snow. Here, kitty, kitty. Please come out from under the sofa." Melinda looked up at Gabe with a feeling of helplessness.

He shrugged. "You heard what Noah and Paul said. Leave the cat be. She'll come out on her own when she's ready."

Melinda released a deep sigh. "That could be hours from now. Snow's just a baby, and she's really scared."

"I'll tell you what," Gabe said as he got to his feet. "Why don't you and me go out on the porch and watch the rain some more? If there's no one in the living room, the cat will be more apt to come out."

She nodded and stood. "You could be right."

Gabe opened the front door, and Melinda followed him outside.

"Sure hope Cinnamon's okay," she murmured. "He's probably as frightened as Snow seems to be."

"Yeah, but he's a wild animal, and I'm sure he'll be fine on his own."

"I suppose. His foot's nearly healed, so he should be okay even if he ran into the woods." Melinda leaned on the porch railing and stared into the yard. "Some party this turned out to be, huh?"

Gabe took a step closer and put his arm around her waist. "It'll be one you won't likely forget, that's for certain sure."

She giggled. "You're right about that."

"Uh—Melinda, I've been wanting to ask you a question."

Her heart started to pound. "What did you want to ask?"

He reached up and stroked the side of her face, and tingles shot all the way up her spine. "I love you, Melinda, and I have for a long time."

She swallowed hard. "I—I love you, too."

"Would you marry me this fall?"

Melinda swallowed around the lump in her throat. She had to think—to stop this roaring rush of emotions and hold on to reason. If she accepted his proposal without telling him about the idea of her becoming a vet, it would be even harder to do later on. *I must tell him now. It can't wait any longer.*

But before she could get the words out, Gabe leaned down and kissed her so tenderly she almost melted into his arms. When the kiss ended, he whispered, "Melinda Andrews, if you marry me, I'll be the happiest man in the world."

Her eyes filled with tears and splashed onto her cheeks. He reached up to wipe them away. "I hope those are tears of joy."

She nodded. "I do want to marry you, Gabe, but—"

"I'm so glad, and I promise to be the best husband in all of Webster County."

He grabbed her hand. "The rain's letting up, so let's take a walk now."

As the rush of water in the drainpipes became mere drops from the eaves, Melinda's resolve to tell Gabe her plans melted away. She would tell him, and soon, but right now all she wanted to do was enjoy this time they had together.

"Jah, okay. We can walk down the driveway a ways," she said.

"Think I'll ask Aaron to be one of my attendants at the wedding," Gabe said as they headed out, hand in hand. "Will you ask Susie?"

Melinda nodded. "Probably so."

"We'll each need one more person to stand up for us. Maybe one of our cousins."

"Uh—there's plenty of time to decide."

"Jah. We won't be published until closer to the wedding, and then once the publication announcement is given at church, we can make the rest of our plans." He squeezed her hand. "I can't wait to make you my wife."

As they walked on, Melinda noticed the misty clouds that seemed to cling to the earth. On both sides of the driveway, leaves lay littered where the wet wind had spun and stuck them in place. It almost seemed if she were in a dream. One that was pleasant and yet made her feel strangely ill at ease. *What would Gabe say if he knew what I was thinking of doing? Would he break our engagement as quickly as he proposed?*

"Did you get everything you wanted for your birthday?" Gabe asked, breaking into her thoughts. "Or is there some secret present you were hoping to get and didn't?"

Melinda wasn't sure how to answer that question. She figured Gabe might like to hear her say that being betrothed to him was her secret present. She was pleased that he'd proposed, and she did want to be his wife, but the truth was, the only secret hidden in her heart was her desire to get more education and become a veterinarian.

"Everyone has some secret they don't want anyone to know about," Gabe went on to say. "But now that you and I are planning to be married, we should be able to tell each other anything. Don't you think?"

"You're right, and I—" Melinda halted.

"What's wrong? What'd you stop walking for?"

"Don't move a muscle."

Gabe froze. "Is there a poisonous snake underfoot?"

She nudged his arm. "Look—aren't they sweet?"

"What?"

"Twin fawns, to your left."

Gabe turned his head just as two young deer walked out of the bushes, not three feet away.

She inched closer to the deer.

"What are you doin'?"

"*Shh . . .*"

Melinda took a few more steps and dropped to her knees. One fawn held back, but the other spotted deer stepped near.

She held her breath. Then the most surprising thing happened. The fawn came right up to her and licked the end of her chin.

Melinda sat very still as both of the deer moved away and disappeared into the brush. She touched the spot on her chin where the fawn had licked. "Did you see that, Gabe?" she murmured. "The little deer gave me a birthday kiss."

nine

Over the next several weeks, Melinda's emotions swung from elation over Gabe's marriage proposal to frustration because she had not yet told him that she was considering leaving the Amish faith to pursue a career in veterinary medicine. She knew she needed to say something soon, because news of their betrothal was bound to get around. And, of course, a few weeks before their wedding, they would be officially published during a church service, then everyone would know.

To make matters worse, Dr. Franklin had recently given Melinda another orphaned raccoon she had named Rhoda, and he continued to tell Melinda what a God-given talent she'd been given when it came to working with animals. Melinda felt that way, too. She cared deeply for all animals, and especially those who needed her help in some way. More and more she felt the pull to become a veterinarian so she could help as many animals as possible. Yet she loved Gabe and wanted to be his wife. She also loved her family and knew how hard it would be if she were to leave them.

As Melinda bent over the rhubarb patch one Friday morning in June, she made a decision. *I must find out if Gabe would be willing to leave the Amish faith with me. If we left together, it would be a little easier, but if I have to do it on my own, I'm not sure I can.*

"Melinda, have you got enough rhubarb yet?"

Grandpa called from the back porch, where he stood with a pot holder in his hand.

Melinda smiled and waved. "Almost. I'll be there with it soon," she called.

Grandpa waved and went back into the house. He was sure doing well these days, and Melinda was glad.

Two weeks ago, Papa Noah and Mama had taken him to see a specialist in Springfield. After numerous tests were run, it had been determined that his loss of memory was due in part to a malfunctioning thyroid. The doctor said it could be treated with medication, which was good news. He also had low blood sugar, which could be controlled by his diet. Those two things, coupled with the fact that Grandpa had never gotten over Grandma's death, had put him in a state of depression and caused some occasional memory loss.

Things would be better now. Grandpa had recently begun helping Mama make jams and preserves to sell at the farmer's market, which seemed to ease his sadness. His mind appeared to be sharper already, too. It was sure a surprise to see Grandpa spending time in the kitchen, though. Melinda remembered how he used to avoid doing anything related to cooking. She had heard him tell Papa Noah how odd he thought it was that his youngest son enjoyed baking so much. But now that he was making delicious jams and jellies, Grandpa acted like he'd been interested in kitchen things for a good long time.

Melinda chuckled to herself "Just goes to show, no one's ever too old to change their mind about things."

A few minutes later, she picked the last stalk of rhubarb and ran up to the house with it. As soon as she had deposited the stalks of rhubarb into the kitchen sink, she headed back outside to check the birdhouse Papa Noah had given her as a birthday present.

"Maybe there will be a note from Gabe," she murmured. It had been several days since she'd last heard from him, and she was anxious to know when they would be going on another date. Seeing him only at their every-other-week preaching services didn't give them any privacy, and they needed to talk without anyone overhearing their conversation. To her knowledge, no one knew about Gabe's proposal yet, and that was a good thing.

Melinda was pleased to hear some baby birds peeping from one end of the double-sided wooden birdhouse, and she was careful not to disturb the little sparrows when she lifted the lid on the side that was now Gabe's and her message box. She was equally pleased to see that a note was waiting for her. It read:

Dear Melinda,

Since the weather has been so warm, I thought it would be nice to go for a drive this evening after supper. Let me know if you'll be free or not. I'll be back to check the message box later this afternoon.

Happily yours,
Gabe

Melinda reached inside the box to retrieve the pencil and tablet they kept there, and she quickly scrawled a note in reply.

Dear Gabe,
*   Tonight should be fine. Come by around seven. I'm looking forward to our time together, as we have some important things to talk about.*
                                          Yours fawnly,
                                          Melinda

"What do you think of this hunk of walnut for the stock of the new gun I'm plannin' to make?" Gabe asked as he held the item in question out for his *daed*'s inspection.

Pap nodded and ran his fingers over the strip of wood. "Looks like it'll work out fine. Always did like to have a hunting gun with a well-made stock."

Gabe smiled. *Maybe this will show him I'm able to make more than simple cabinets, birdhouses, and feeders.*

"You plannin' to do some huntin' this fall?" his father questioned.

"Yep, and I hope to use my new gun."

"Sounds gut, but any huntin' you want to do will have to be on your day off or after the shop is closed for the day." Pap picked up a stack of work orders and quickly thumbed through them. "We need to get busy with these jobs. You'll have to work on your gun stock during your free time, too."

Gabe frowned but set the piece of wood aside. If he worked on his own projects after hours, he would have less time to court Melinda.

He thought about the note he had left her earlier, saying he would be by this evening to take her for a buggy ride.

Guess I could run over to her place during lunch and leave her another note saying I can't take her for a ride after all. Gabe pondered the idea a moment, then shook his head. *No way! Melinda comes first. Hunting season is several months away. I can work on the gun stock some other time.*

Melinda had just started setting the table for supper when Papa Noah entered the kitchen with a worried expression on his face.

"Where's your mamm?" he asked.

"Over at Grandpa Hertzler's side of the house. They're finishing up with the rhubarb-strawberry jam they've been making today."

"Do you know if we've got any hydrogen peroxide in the house?"

"I think there's some in the cupboard above the sink. What do you need it for?"

"The new horse I bought a few days ago has a cut on her back leg. Thought I'd have to call the vet at first, but the cut ain't too deep, so I think it's somethin' I can tend to myself."

"She didn't have a cut leg when you bought her, I hope."

He shook his head and ambled across the room to the cupboard. "I think she may have gouged it on the fence. Probably tryin' to get out."

Melinda felt immediate concern. "She's not happy here? Is that what you think, Papa Noah?"

He pulled the bottle of peroxide down and turned around. "Looks like it. If I had more free time to spend with her, she might feel calmer and at home already. Between my job at the tree farm and all the chores I have to do here, there ain't enough hours in the day."

Melinda placed the last glass on the table and moved toward her stepfather. "I could do it, Papa Noah. I'm good with animals—you know that."

"Of course you are, but I don't think—"

"Please, let me try," Melinda begged. "I'll show Nellie some attention so she learns to like it here, and I'll tend that cut on her leg. She'll be good as new in no time."

Papa Noah's furrowed brows let her know he was at least thinking on the idea.

"I'll squeeze it in between chores here and my job at the veterinary clinic." Melinda clasped his arm. "Please, Papa Noah."

He smiled and handed her the bottle of peroxide. "Okay, then, you can start right now."

Melinda sprinted for the door. "Tell Mama I've got the propane turned on low, and I'll be back in time to help her serve the stew that's cooking for supper."

Gabe whistled the whole way over to Melinda's house. He sure hoped she could go for a buggy ride, because he could hardly wait to spend time with her and talk about their future. The summer months would go by quickly, then soon it would be time for their wedding. Of course, they hadn't set a date yet, so he didn't know if it would be this fall or if Melinda would prefer to wait until next spring.

"I want it to be soon, but if I just had my own business, I'd feel more prepared," he mumbled. "Wonder how long I'll have to keep workin' for Pap before I have enough money saved up to go out on my own." He had looked at a couple of places to rent, but the owners of the buildings were asking too much, and he didn't think Pap would take to the idea of him building a shop right there on the same property as his place of business.

I just need to be patient and pray about this more, Gabe decided.

When he pulled into the Hertzlers' front yard a short time later, he spotted Isaiah on the lawn playing with his beagle hound, Jericho.

The boy waved, and Gabe lifted a hand in response. "Where's Melinda? I hope she's ready for our date."

Isaiah turned his palms upward. "Don't know nothin' about no date, but Melinda's out in the barn with Papa's new horse."

Gabe figured she had gone there to pass the time while she waited for him. He guided his horse to the hitching rail and pulled on the reins. Then he jumped down, secured the animal, and headed for the barn.

Gabe found Melinda in one of the stalls on her knees

80

next to a nice-looking gray and white mare. "Are you ready for our ride?" he called.

She stood and smoothed the wrinkles in her long green dress. "Oh, Gabe, I don't think I can go with you tonight."

"Didn't you get my note?"

"I did, and I wrote you one in return."

His face warmed. "Uh—I forgot to check the birdhouse on my way in. What did your note say?"

"It said I could go, but now something's come up." She pointed to the horse. "As you can see, Nellie has a cut on her back leg, and I tended it before supper."

Gabe opened his mouth to say something, but she chopped off his sentence.

"The mare's been acting kind of spooky and hasn't adjusted to her new surroundings yet, so after we ate, I came back to the barn to see that she remains calm and doesn't start her wound bleeding again."

Gabe folded his arms as they exchanged pointed stares. He knew his was angry, but hers seemed defensive.

"I hope you understand," she said with a lift of her chin.

"I don't."

"Have you no concern for Papa Noah's horse?"

"It's not that I don't care. I just don't see why it's your job to nursemaid her. Shouldn't the vet be doin' that?"

Melinda stroked the horse's ears. "If the cut were deeper and needed stitches, Papa Noah would have called Dr. Franklin. But it's not that bad, which is why he asked me to tend Nellie's leg."

"That's fine," Gabe said through tight lips, "but how is stayin' here gonna help her?"

Melinda left the stall and moved to his side. "The horse is calmer when I'm with her, and I'm just starting to gain some headway."

Gabe shrugged as frustration and disappointment boiled inside his chest. "Sure, whatever. If your daed's horse is more important than me, then I guess that's just the way it is." He turned and started to walk away, but she reached out and touched his arm.

"Please don't leave mad. You could stay and help me with the horse."

He swung around. "I can't believe you'd expect me to spend this warm summer evening cooped up in the barn with a sweaty animal."

Tears gathered in the corners of Melinda's eyes, and they were nearly Gabe's undoing. He hadn't meant to make her cry. Hadn't meant to be so harsh or unwilling to help. One of the things that had originally attracted him to Melinda was her caring attitude and sensitivity toward hurting animals, and now he was scolding her for it.

He pulled her into his arms. "I'm sorry, Melinda. Let's not fight, okay?"

She sniffed. "I don't want to, Gabe. I want us to always be happy. But if you don't understand my desire to work with animals, I don't see how—"

He stopped her rush of words with a kiss, and any shred of anger he had felt earlier fell away like wood chips beneath the sander. "I love you so much, Melinda."

"I love you, too."

"How about tomorrow night? Think you can go for a buggy ride with me then?"

She nodded. "I hope so."

Gabe kissed her again, then motioned toward the horse's stall. "How 'bout if I stay and help you cross tie the horse so she won't move around so much?"

"I would appreciate it."

"Maybe when we're done we can sit and talk awhile."

She grinned up at him. "That would be wunderbaar."

ten

Melinda sat at the kitchen table reading a passage of scripture from her Bible out loud. Jesus said, "Peace I leave with you, my peace I give unto you: not as the world giveth, give I unto you. Let not your heart be troubled, neither let it be afraid."

She closed her eyes. *In my heart there is no peace, Lord. Help me make this agonizing decision about becoming a vet, and give me the courage and opportunity to speak with Gabe about it tonight on our buggy ride. I really can't decide what I should do until I know how he feels about things.*

Melinda knew she should have told him last night when they'd spent time in the barn with Nellie. But after having that one disagreement, she'd been afraid to bring up anything that might cause more dissension.

"Are you about ready to help me and Grandpa make jam?" Mama asked, interrupting Melinda's thoughts. "He would like us to go over to his place as soon as we can."

Melinda nodded. "I'll be able to help for a while, but Dr. Franklin needs me at the clinic this afternoon."

"That should work. I'm sure we can get most of it done by noon."

Melinda stood and had just closed her Bible when Isaiah bolted through the back door grinning from ear to ear. "Look what I found!" He held out his hands.

Their mother's face turned pale, and she trembled. "Isaiah Hertzler, get that snake out of my house!"

He glanced at the reptile and frowned. "It's dead, Mama. Found it down in the root cellar, and it wasn't movin' a lick."

"So that was a reason to bring the creature in here?"

"I don't see why you're afraid of a dead garter snake. It can't hurt ya none."

"Isaiah—" Mama's tone was one of warning, and Melinda held her breath and waited to see what her little brother would do.

"All right, all right." Isaiah turned toward the door but suddenly whirled back around. "I'm thirsty and need a glass of water. I'll get one real quick and be gone, okay?" Without waiting for his mother's reply, he plopped the snake on the floor, grabbed a glass from the cupboard, and headed for the kitchen sink. He had no more than turned on the faucet when Mama's shrill scream ricocheted off the walls.

Melinda's attention was immediately drawn to the creature Isaiah had dropped. Not only was the snake very much alive, but it was now slithering across the linoleum toward the table.

Mama hollered again and jumped onto a chair. Isaiah laughed until tears rolled down his cheeks.

"It's not funny," Mama said, shaking her finger. "I want you to pick up that snake and haul it back outside where it belongs."

Isaiah took a few steps backward and shook his head. "No way! I ain't about to touch him."

"Why not?"

"He might bite me."

"You weren't worried about that when you lugged him into the house."

"I thought he was dead."

"Garter snakes aren't poisonous," Melinda put in.

"Maybe not, but its bite could still hurt," Isaiah retorted.

"If you're not going to do as I say, then go on up to your room. And don't come out until I say you can," Mama said sternly.

Isaiah frowned. "But that might be hours from now."

"Would you rather receive a *bletching?*"

"No, Mama." He hurried from the room.

Melinda could hardly believe her brother was acting like such a baby. If she'd been Mama, she would have given him that spanking she had threatened.

With a shake of her head, she bent down and grabbed ahold of the snake.

"Melinda, what do you think you're doing?" Mama's voice quavered, and her eyes were huge.

"I'm going to take the critter outside where it belongs."

Her mother looked unsure for a moment but finally nodded.

Once Melinda was outside and a good distance from the house, she set the snake on the ground, and it slithered off toward the woods.

She stood there a few seconds, staring at the stately pine trees behind their place and breathing in the fresh outdoor scent. *I wish I didn't have to go back inside and help Mama and Grandpa make jam. I'd much rather spend my morning in the woods where I could draw and watch for deer.* Melinda sighed and turned around.

With a feeling of anticipation, Gabe headed down the road in his buggy toward the Hertzlers' place. He'd been busy in the shop all day and hadn't been able to get away long enough to leave Melinda a note to confirm their buggy ride.

"Sure hope she's not still doctoring that horse's leg," he muttered. He'd been miffed the night before when she turned down a ride in his buggy to be with her daed's horse, but Melinda's tears had caused him to back down. He did feel a little better about the fact that she had agreed to see him tonight.

When Gabe pulled into the Hertzlers', he halted his horse, jumped down from the buggy, and hitched the gelding to the rail near the barn. A few seconds later, he stood on the front porch, ready to knock on the screen door. But before Gabe could raise his knuckles, he heard loud voices coming from inside the house.

"Melinda, how many times have we told you about bringin' your critters into the house?" Gabe recognized Noah's voice, and he sounded upset.

"Only your kitten is allowed inside," Faith chimed in.

"I've told her that already, but then she don't ever listen to nothin' I have to say," Melinda's little brother added.

If Melinda's folks are mad at her, she probably won't be allowed to go out with me. Chilly fingers of dread wound their way through Gabe's middle. Would he suffer another disappointment tonight? *Maybe I should turn around and head back home.*

"Reba and Rhoda were fighting in the cage they share," he heard Melinda say.

"Why wasn't Reba in her own cage?" her stepfather questioned.

"The latch won't stay shut, and she keeps chewing the wire and getting out, the same way Cinnamon the squirrel did the night of my birthday party."

Gabe drew in a deep breath and blew it out quickly. *I knew I should have had a talk with her about releasing that raccoon into the woods. I'd better see if I can help in some way.*

He lifted his hand and knocked on the edge of the screen door.

"Someone's at the front door," Isaiah announced. "Want me to see who it is?"

"It's probably Gabe," Melinda said, moving in that direction. "He said he'd be coming over tonight to take me for a buggy ride."

Mama frowned. "What about the raccoon? She belongs outside."

"Can I at least answer the door?"

"Jah, sure. If it's Gabe, maybe he can help capture the critter." Papa Noah's face was red as a cherry tomato, and a trickle of sweat rolled down his forehead. They had all been in on the chase to catch Reba, but so far she had escaped everyone's grasp.

Melinda rushed to the door and was glad to see Gabe standing on the porch.

"I came to pick you up for our buggy ride, but I have a notion this isn't such a good time."

"We've been trying to catch one of my raccoons," she explained.

His eyebrows rose. "Seems like every time I come over here you're either chasin' some critter or tendin' to one."

"It has been kind of hectic lately," Melinda admitted, opening the screen door for him. "Come on in. Maybe you can help us catch Reba."

"If you do catch the coon, are you plannin' to let it go?"

She tipped her head. "Go?"

"Yeah. Release it into the woods."

"I can't do that, Gabe. Reba's half blind, and she needs to be somewhere safe."

"What about the other raccoon?"

"Rhoda's an orphan, too."

"But she's not sick or anything?"

"No."

"Then why not let her go free?"

"Because she's been keeping Reba company."

Gabe released a huff and stepped into the house just as the raccoon darted into the living room from the door leading to the hallway. Before Melinda had time to respond, the coon snatched one of her mother's slippers, growling and shaking it like a dog would.

Melinda bent down and grabbed one end of the slipper, tugging it free from Reba's mouth. Gabe came around behind the animal and nearly had it in his grasp when Melinda's cat showed up on the scene. Reba growled. Snow hissed. Then each of them took off in opposite directions.

Melinda watched in horror as the raccoon darted around the living room, bumping into pieces of furniture and acting disoriented.

"What's wrong with that coon?" Gabe asked, scratching the side of his head. "It's carrying on like it's been drinking hard cider or something."

"As I said before, Reba has limited vision." Melinda pursed her lips. "She does seem to be able to follow movement, though."

Gabe snapped his fingers. "That's good news. Open the front door, and I'll see if I can get the critter to follow me outside."

"I'll help you, Gabe," Papa Noah said when he

entered the room, followed by Mama and Isaiah.

Melinda wasn't sure Gabe's plan would work, but she figured she should be prepared just in case. "Let me go out to the barn and get Reba's cage. If she does run out the door, I'll need to be ready for her."

"Okay, but hurry," Mama said, fanning her flushed face with her hands.

A few minutes later, Melinda stood on the front porch holding the cage. She set it in front of the door and hollered, "Okay. I'm ready!"

Mama held the door open, and as Melinda watched the scene unfold, she didn't know who looked funnier—the raccoon, who continued to bump into things, or the menfolk, as they took turns diving after her.

After several more attempts, Reba was finally ushered out the door and into the cage. Relieved that the chase had ended at last, Melinda flopped into a chair and doubled over with laughter.

"I don't see what's so humorous." Mama frowned. "This is the second time in a month one of your critters has gotten into the house and caused an uproar."

"Your mamm's right," Papa Noah added firmly. "This kind of commotion has got to stop."

Melinda was tempted to remind her folks that she wasn't the only one in the family responsible for bringing animals inside, but she didn't want to say anything disrespectful. She glanced over at Gabe, hoping he would say something on her behalf, but he merely stood there with a placid look on his face.

"Gabe and I had planned to go for a buggy ride," she said. "That's why he dropped by."

Her mother shook her head. "Until you can find some way to keep your animals locked in their cages, you won't be going anywhere to socialize."

"But, Mama, that's not fair—"

"And neither is tearing up the house," Papa Noah said. "You're nineteen years old, Melinda, which means you should be more responsible." He frowned. "And one more thing: as long as you're livin' under our roof, you'll do as we say. Is that clear?"

She hung her head and blinked back tears. One crept from the corner of her eye and into her hairline, and she wiped it away. "Yes, Papa Noah."

Melinda felt a little better when Gabe reached over and clasped her hand in his. "Not to worry," he whispered in a comforting voice. "As soon as I get home, I'm going to make some new locks for your animal cages."

eleven

Melinda was on her way to Seymour to deliver some jars of Grandpa's rhubarb-strawberry jam to the owner of the bed and breakfast there when she decided to stop and see Gabe. She hoped he'd found the time to make some new locks for her cages like he'd promised, because as long as her animals kept getting out, her folks would be irritated and might ask her to stop taking in strays altogether.

When she pulled up to Swartz's Woodworking Shop and hopped down from the buggy, she noticed Gabe's mother in her vegetable garden holding a hoe.

"Nice day, isn't it?" Leah called.

"Jah, very pretty."

"Have you got a minute?"

Melinda headed up the driveway and joined Gabe's mother at the edge of her garden. "It looks like things are growing well. How are you able to keep up with all the weeds?" She knew Gabe's parents were both in their sixties and figured with no children except Gabe living at home, it would be harder to get things done.

Leah pushed a wayward strand of grayish-brown hair away from her flushed face. "As you know, two of my daughters, Karen and Lydia, live nearby. They often drop over with their kinner, and everyone helps me weed."

Melinda did a mental head count. Leah and Stephen Swartz had five children and twenty grandchildren, and since all of their offspring were still young enough to have more kinner, they could likely end up with several more *kinskinner.* She wondered if she and Gabe would be blessed with many children when they got married. *If we get married,* she thought ruefully. *What if he won't go English with me?*

Melinda had pretty well decided that was what she wanted to do. With her folks not understanding her need to care for animals, and even refusing to let her go out with Gabe, Melinda figured it would be best if she did leave home and pursue a career in veterinary medicine. Besides, the longer she worked for Dr. Franklin, the more she desired to be a vet. It would mean great sacrifice and a lot more schooling, but she had convinced herself it was God's will. Now if she could only convince Gabe.

"I've got a question for you," Leah said, bringing Melinda's thoughts to a halt.

"What is it?"

"I know you work at the vet's and care for lots of animals at home."

"Jah."

"Well, I've been havin' some trouble with deer gettin' into my garden and wondered if you had any ideas on keepin' them out."

Melinda knew firsthand that the deer and other wildlife in the area could take over a garden if certain measures weren't taken. She also knew some folks used that as an excuse to shoot the deer.

"The best thing would be to build a tall fence, but we've had good luck by hanging tin cans around our garden so that when the wind blows, they make noise," she said. "My mamm has also shaved strong-smelling soap around the outside of the garden, and another idea would be to put some feed out for the deer close to the edge of your property. If they're getting enough to eat, they won't be as likely to bother your garden."

Leah smiled. "I appreciate the suggestions. You're real smart, Melinda."

"Danki." Melinda glanced toward the woodworking

shop, which was on the west side of the Swartz property.

"Well, I won't keep you any longer. I'm sure you came to visit my son, and if I know Gabe, he'll be pleased as anything to see you."

Melinda nodded. "I did want to speak with him. Guess I'll head out to the shop now."

"Tell my son I'll have lunch ready in an hour or so."

"Okay. It was nice talking to you, Leah."

"Same here."

A few minutes later, Melinda entered the woodworking shop and spotted Gabe sanding a cabinet door. "Nice job you're doing," she said with a smile.

"Danki." He set the sandpaper aside and leaned on his workbench. "Say, you're just the person I was hopin' to see today."

She felt a warm sensation spread over her face. "That's nice to know."

"I haven't had enough free time yet to make new cages, but I have been able to make a couple of new doors for the cages you already have," Gabe said. "Thought if it was okay, I'd bring them by your house this evening and test 'em on your sneaky raccoons."

"That would be great," Melinda said with a burst of enthusiasm. "I'll be home all evening, so feel free to come by anytime after supper."

"Where are you headed to now, or did you just drive down this way to see me?" he asked with a quick wink.

She grinned. "I did come by to see you, but I'm also

on my way to Seymour to take some of Grandpa's jam to the bed and breakfast. The owners will probably serve some of it to their customers, and I think they're planning to sell a few jars in their gift shop."

"That's gut. Glad your grandpa is doin' better these days and has found an outlet for his jam." Gabe motioned to the door. "My daed's outside cuttin' a stack of lumber that was delivered yesterday afternoon. I think he's planning to head for Seymour later on. He has some finished cabinets he wants to deliver to an English woman who works for the chiropractor there."

Melinda made a sweeping gesture with her hand. "If they look anything like the ones I see here in the shop, I'm sure she'll be real pleased."

"Yep." Gabe blew the sandpaper dust off the cabinet, and it trickled through the air, causing Melinda to sneeze.

"*Gott segen eich*—God bless you," Gabe said with a look of concern. "Sorry for sending all that dust in your direction."

"I'm all right."

"Guess you'll have to get used to sandpaper dust if you're plannin' to marry a carpenter." He glanced around nervously. Was he about to kiss her?

"Gabe—there's—uh—something I need to tell you."

"What is it, Melinda? Are you having second thoughts about marrying me?"

"No, it's not that."

"What is it, then?"

She was about to reply, but Gabe's father stepped into the room. "Herman Yutzy's here to pick up his table and chairs," he announced. "I need your help loadin' them into his wagon, Gabe."

"Jah, okay." Gabe wiggled his eyebrows at Melinda. "Duty calls."

"That's all right. I need to get to Seymour anyhow. See you this evening, Gabe."

"You can count on it."

When Melinda arrived home later that day, she was greeted with a sorrowful sight. Isaiah's dog had gone on the rampage, killing a female rabbit that had gotten out of her cage. Melinda was sure it happened because the door wouldn't stay latched. She was heartsick when she discovered the dead rabbit's four orphaned babies, knowing they might not survive without their mother.

"I'll need to feed them," she murmured, reaching into the open cage.

"Sorry about this," Isaiah said, stepping up beside her. "Don't know what came over Jericho to do such a thing."

"If you kept him tied up like I've asked you to do, he wouldn't have had the opportunity." Melinda lifted the rabbits gently out of the cage and placed them inside a cardboard box. "I'll take them into the house where I can better care for their needs."

"Mama won't like it," Isaiah asserted. "She's gettin'

sick of your critters and the messes they make."

Melinda wrinkled her nose. "Jah, well, you'd best let me worry about that." She left the barn before her brother could offer a retort.

When she stepped onto the back porch a few minutes later, she spotted Grandpa sitting in the wicker rocking chair outside his living quarters. He waved at her. "Did ya get all my jars of jam delivered?"

She nodded. "Every last one is gone."

"Then what have ya got in the box?"

"Four baby rabbits." Melinda moved closer to his chair and held out the box so he could take a look. "Isaiah's dog killed the mother. Now it's my job to save them."

Grandpa fingered his long white beard. "It doesn't surprise me that you'd be willin' to do that. You're such a caring young woman."

She leaned over and kissed his wrinkled cheek. "I'd best get these little ones inside and find a way to feed them."

"I hope they make it."

"Me, too." Melinda opened the back door and stepped into the house.

That evening after supper, Melinda sat on the front porch swing, waiting for Gabe to show up. She had just fed the orphaned bunnies with an eyedropper and put them back inside the cardboard box where she planned to keep them for the time being.

A slight breeze had come up, whisking away some

of the oppressive muggy air that had hovered over the land most of the day. It was already July, and soon August would be here. More warm weather would likely follow and last far into fall.

A horse and buggy trotted into the yard about then, and Melinda smiled. It was Gabe. She left the porch and hurried out to greet him.

Gabe climbed down from his buggy and retrieved two wooden cage doors from the back. He nodded toward the barn. "Let's go see how they work, shall we?"

As soon as they entered the barn, Melinda took Reba and Rhoda out of their cages and placed them inside an empty horse stall. Gabe removed the old cage doors, which Melinda had wired shut. Soon he had the new doors set in place.

"The latches can't be jimmied from the inside," he explained. "I don't think the coons will be able to escape, and as soon as I find the time, I'll make you a couple of cages with doors like these."

"That would be wunderbaar." Melinda retrieved Reba and Rhoda and put them in their respective cages.

Gabe closed the doors and clicked the locks shut. "I dare either one of you critters to get out now," he said, squinting at the animals.

"If it keeps them in, I'll be happy, and so will my folks."

Gabe lifted Melinda's chin with his thumb and lowered his head. His lips were just inches from hers when her brother burst into the barn. "Yodel-oh-de-tee! Yodel-oh-de-tee! My mama taught me how to yodel when I sat on her knee. . . ." Isaiah halted when he saw Gabe and Melinda, and his face turned red. "Oops. Didn't know anyone was in here."

"And I didn't know you could yodel," Gabe said. "I thought only Melinda and your mamm were the yodelers in the family."

"He can't yodel." Melinda tapped her foot impatiently. "He just does that to mimic me."

Isaiah stuck out his tongue. "Do not. I came to the barn to see if Jericho was here."

Melinda clenched her teeth. "That mutt had better not be running free again."

"He can't be chained up all the time, and it's not his fault your goofy pets are always gettin' out of their cages."

"I think that problem's been solved," Gabe said before Melinda could respond. "I just put new doors with better locks on the coons' cages, and if it keeps 'em in, I'll be making more cages for Melinda's other critters."

Isaiah peered at Reba's cage door. "If Papa ever gets around to buildin' Jericho a dog run, maybe you can put a door like this on his cage."

Melinda poked her brother's arm. "Is that any way to ask a favor? Gabe doesn't have a lot of time on his hands and shouldn't be expected to make you a cage door."

"I'll make the time for that," Gabe said with a wide

smile. "Fact is, I'll build the whole dog run for Jericho, and it will give me a chance to make something on my own without Pap lookin' over my shoulder and tellin' me how it's done. Not only that, but it will keep your dog from hurting Melinda's critters."

Before her little brother could comment, Melinda moved toward the barn door. "Come on, Gabe. Let's go tell my folks about the cage doors and see if they mind if we go for a buggy ride."

twelve

Melinda drew in a deep breath and prayed for the courage to say what had been on her mind for weeks. Gabe deserved to know, and now was the time to tell him.

"I've been wanting to discuss something with you," she said as they headed down Highway C in his open buggy.

"What's on your mind?"

Melinda moistened her lips with the tip of her tongue. "You know how much I enjoy working with animals."

"Jah."

"And I want to help as many of the sick and hurting ones as I can."

He nodded.

"Well, the thing is—" This was going to be harder than she had expected. No wonder she'd put off telling him for so long.

"The thing is, what?" Gabe prompted.

She drew in a deep breath and started again. "Dr. Franklin says I have a special way with animals—a God-given talent."

"He's right about that, Melinda. Look how well your daed's horse has responded to you. And those baby bunnies are doin' well under your care, too. Animals have a sixth sense and know when a human being cares for them."

Melinda felt relief that Gabe realized her capabilities and saw how she interacted with the animals she had taken under her wing. Maybe he would be receptive to the idea of her becoming a vet.

"I do care a lot," she admitted, "but unfortunately, I'm not able to do as much for wounded or sick animals as I would like."

"That's why Doc Franklin's available," Gabe said, flicking the reins to get his horse moving a bit faster. "When you find an ailing critter or one somebody's brought over to your place that has more wrong with it than you can handle, you take it to the vet."

Melinda clasped her hands tightly in her lap. *Help me, Lord. Give me the right words.*

"Well, if that don't beat all," Gabe said pointing to the other side of the road. "It's another dead *hasch*. Probably some car or a truck ran into it."

Melinda flinched. She hated to see dead deer, whether they were lying alongside the road after being hit by a car or hanging in someone's barn during deer hunting season.

"If the deer aren't thinned enough during hunting season," Gabe said, "they overpopulate and will soon overrun our area." He motioned to the deer they had just passed. "I'd rather see 'em shot for meat than go to waste thataway, wouldn't you?"

Melinda didn't reply at first. She wanted to be sure Gabe didn't take anything she had to say in the wrong way. Then finally, taking in a quick breath, she said, "I don't like to see any deer killed, Gabe. We raise hogs, sheep, and cows for food, so why would anyone need to kill the deer?"

He shrugged. "Some in our community prefer the taste of deer meat, and even if we do have other animals to butcher, it's nice to have a change."

Melinda didn't like the way this conversation was going, and she decided to get back to the subject of her becoming a veterinarian. "Dr. Franklin thinks I have what it takes to become a vet," she blurted out.

Gabe stared straight ahead, as though he were either mulling things over or trying to stay focused on the road. The buggy rolled along, and the horse's hooves made a steady *clip-clop* against the pavement, but he remained quiet.

Melinda reached over and touched Gabe's arm. "Awhile back, the doctor gave me some information on the necessary college courses I would need to take, and he told me about a couple different schools of veterinary medicine."

Gabe jerked unexpectedly on the reins and guided his horse and buggy to the side of the road. When they were stopped, he turned in his seat and stared at Melinda. "Just how far have you gone with all this? Have you already made up your mind to leave the Amish faith? Have you made application to a college?"

She shook her head. "No, no. I would need to get my GED first, and then—"

"So you have decided."

"Not yet, but Dr. Franklin says if I want something badly enough, I should be willing to make whatever sacrifices are necessary. Even if it means giving up those things that are dear to me in order to reach my goal."

"If you were to get the training you needed to become a vet, it would mean leaving behind the Amish faith and everyone you love." Gabe's eyes were downcast, and his shoulders slumped. Apparently he thought this would mean the end of their relationship.

Melinda clasped his hand. "I wouldn't have to leave you, Gabe. Not if you'd be willing to leave here with me."

"What?" His mouth dropped open. "How could you even suggest such a thing?"

"I—I just thought if you loved me—"

She noticed a vein in Gabe's temple had begun to throb. "You know I love you, Melinda, but I'm happy livin' here, and I don't want to leave the Amish faith." He squinted as he stared at her long and hard. "I can't imagine you wanting to leave, either."

"I don't want to leave, but in order to—"

"I asked you once if you ever missed the English world or thought you would want to go back to it someday, and you said you were happy being Amish."

"I am happy being Amish, but I can't become a veterinarian and remain part of our faith."

"So I guess that means you'll have to choose between me and the modern world."

Frustration welled up in Melinda's soul, and she fought to keep her emotions under control.

"It's not the modern world I would be choosing, Gabe. Becoming a vet would mean I could help so many animals, and—"

"You're helpin' some now, aren't you?"

"Jah, but in such a small way."

He shrugged. "Seems to me that you oughta be happy with what you can do for the animals you've taken in and quit wishin' for somethin' that goes against our beliefs."

She lowered her head. "I'm not sure becoming a vet goes against *my* beliefs."

Gabe grabbed hold of Melinda's arms and gave her a gentle shake. "You've been baptized and have joined the church. You've made a vow to God to adhere to our church rules. If you left to become one with the world, you would be shunned. Have you thought about the seriousness of that?"

"Of course I have, and it would hurt to leave my family behind." More tears seeped out from under her lashes, and she swallowed around the constriction in her throat.

"What do your folks have to say about all this, Melinda? Are they letting you go with their bless-ings?"

She shook her head. "I haven't told them yet. I wanted to discuss it with you first and see if you would be willing to—"

"No! I won't leave the Amish faith." Gabe's pained expression softened some, and he squeezed her arms gently but firmly. "I've been working real hard and savin' up money so I can start my own place of busi-ness. I'm doin' it for us so I can make a good living and provide for the family I'd hoped we would have."

Confusion swirled in Melinda's brain like a tornado at full speed. She did love Gabe, but if he wouldn't leave the Amish faith, then she would be completely on her own if she decided to get the necessary schooling to become a vet. And how would she pay for her classes? She knew college was expensive, not to mention the additional training at a veterinary school. What she made working for Dr. Franklin wasn't nearly enough, and she sure couldn't ask her folks to help out.

Melinda squeezed her eyes shut. *I guess that was a selfish thought. I'm not asking Gabe to leave the Amish faith so he can help me financially. I want him to support my decision because he loves me and wants to be with me no matter which world I choose to live in.*

She opened her eyes and looked at him. "Would you do me one favor, Gabe?"

"What's that?"

"Would you at least pray about the matter?"

His forehead wrinkled as his eyebrows drooped. "You want me to pray about you becoming a vet?"

She nodded. "And ask God what His plans for you might be."

Gabe sat there awhile staring straight ahead. Then finally, he gathered up the reins. "I will pray about this, but I think right now I'd best take you home. I don't feel like riding any further or talking more about our future."

"Me neither." Melinda placed her hand on his shoulder. "Oh, and Gabe—"

"Jah?"

"Please don't say anything to my folks or anyone else about what we've discussed this evening, okay?"

He gave a quick nod. "It ain't my place to do the tellin'. I'll leave that up to you."

thirteen

Melinda stood in front of the birdhouse out by their driveway reading the note she had just discovered from Gabe.

Dear Melinda,

I spoke with your daed yesterday, and he said it would be fine if I want to help Isaiah build a dog run since he still hasn't found the time. He also said he thought I'd do a much better job than he could, seein' as how I'm a carpenter and have all the skills and proper tools.

So I plan to come by after work today and begin the project. If you've nothing else to do, maybe you can keep me company. If not, then we might get in a few minutes to visit when I'm done for the day.

Always yours,
Gabe

Melinda frowned as she tucked the note inside the front of her apron. He hadn't said a word about her becoming a vet or made any mention of whether he'd been praying about their situation or not. Maybe he planned to discuss it with her tonight. That could be why he mentioned her keeping him company or having a few minutes to visit when he was done at the end of the day.

Melinda bent down and picked up her cat, who had been sunning herself on the grass. "You've got life made, ya know that, Snow?"

Snow's only response was a soft *meow.*

"I wish all I had to do was lie around and soak up the sun."

"You wouldn't be happy, and you know it."

Melinda looked up at the sound of her grandfather's mellow voice. He sat in his favorite wicker rocking chair on the front porch snapping green beans into a plastic bowl wedged between his knees.

"You're right, Grandpa. I wouldn't be happy if I

wasn't busy," she said as she stepped up beside him. "I enjoy caring for my animals too much to sit around all day and do nothing."

"Speaking of your animals . . . Have you let any of the wild ones go lately?"

She nodded and flopped into the chair beside him, nestling Snow in her lap. "In all fairness to Rhoda, the healthy raccoon, I released her the other day." She sighed. "But now Reba is really lonely without her."

"Maybe you should let her go, too."

"I can't. As you know, the raccoon's partially blind, and I'm sure she wouldn't make it on her own in the woods." Melinda stroked the cat behind its left ear. "Gabe's coming over later to help Isaiah build a dog run, so maybe once my brother's mutt is locked away, I can let Reba roam around our place whenever I'm at home and can keep an eye out for her."

Grandpa's bushy white eyebrows drew together. "You think it's fair to confine Isaiah's dog so your raccoon can run free?"

Melinda shrugged. "I suppose not, but Jericho's been known to attack other animals, too. Don't forget the baby bunnies I'm taking care of. Jericho killed their mother."

"That was a shame, but the dog's only doin' what comes natural to him. Maybe when Gabe's done with the dog run, he can build some other kind of pen for the coon."

Melinda leaned forward. "You mean something bigger than the cage I keep her in now?"

"Jah. Maybe he could make it more like the cages I've seen at the zoo." Grandpa dropped another bean into the bowl. "Some of those zoo cages are real nice—tree branches, scrub brush, and small pools of water inside."

Melinda's heart started to pound as a host of ideas skittered through her mind. How wunderbaar it would be if she had larger cages that were similar to the animals' natural habitat. The critters would feel more at home until it was time to let them go free.

Why am I even thinking such thoughts? If I leave home to go to college, I won't be caring for any of my forest animal friends until I become a vet, and then it will be in a much different way. She blew out her breath. *That could be several years from now.*

Gabe clucked to his horse to get him moving faster. He was tired after a long day at the shop but looked forward to going over to the Hertzlers' to build the dog run for Isaiah. It would be something different to work on for a change, and he'd have a chance to speak with Melinda. Maybe he could talk some sense into her and make her see more clearly what the consequences would be if she left the Amish faith.

He thought about his own plans to open a woodworking shop where he could make a variety of things. *What would be the point in doing that if Melinda leaves and I stay behind? Without her by my side, nothing will be the same.*

When Gabe pulled into the Hertzlers' yard, he

parked his buggy next to the barn. Since he would be there a few hours, he decided to unhitch the horse and put him in one of the stalls.

As he led the gelding through the barn door, he spotted Melinda on the other side of the building in front of an animal cage with her back to him.

He hurried to get the horse situated in a stall, then strolled over to where she stood. "Hey! What are you up to?"

As soon as Melinda turned around, Gabe saw that she held a raccoon in her arms.

"You shouldn't carry that coon around like that," he admonished, wishing he had said something sooner about her taking such chances. "What if the critter bites or scratches you real bad?"

Melinda lifted her chin and looked at him as if he'd taken leave of his senses. "Reba's as tame as my cat, and she likes it when I hold her."

"Humph! She's a wild animal. Never know what she might do."

"I don't want to argue with you, Gabe. I've been taking in wild animals since I was a young girl, and I think I know what I'm doing."

Gabe blew out his breath. She was right; they shouldn't be arguing. Besides, his irritation had more to do with what she had told him about wanting to leave the Amish faith and becoming a vet than it did with the silly raccoon.

"Sorry," he mumbled. "Didn't mean to upset you."

"All's forgiven." She put Reba back in her cage and

turned to face him. "I was wondering if you've thought any more about what we discussed the other night."

He glanced around. "Are we alone?"

She nodded. "Papa Noah's still at work, Mama and Grandpa are inside the house, and the last time I saw Isaiah, he was digging in the dirt out behind the barn."

Gabe plunked down on a bale of straw, and Melinda seated herself beside him. "In answer to your question," he said, "I have thought more about it, and I've also been praying."

"That's gut. Have you made a decision?"

"I'm hopin' you'll change your mind and decide to be content with being Amish."

She frowned. "I am content being Amish. I'm just not content with being unable to properly care for any animals I find that are hurt."

"So what it boils down to is that one of us has to give up something we feel is important in order for us to be together."

Melinda opened her mouth, but he rushed on. "If you leave home to get the schooling you'd need to become a vet, and I go with you, then I'll be giving up a way of life that I love. And if you stay Amish to please me, then you'll be givin' up your desire to care for more animals in a better way than you're doin' now."

She nodded. "That's true, but if I leave home, I'll also be giving up my family and the way of life I've become accustomed to, same as you. So sacrifices would have to be made on both our parts if we decided to go English."

Gabe massaged the bridge of his nose as he contemplated their problem. As far as he was concerned, it was a no-win situation, and no matter how it turned out, one of them would be unhappy.

"We don't have to make a decision right now," Melinda said patting his arm. "However, I need to get registered for classes at the college in Springfield before the end of August, and in the meantime, I'm going to see about getting my graduate equivalency diploma—GED."

He shook his head slowly. "Your folks would really be upset if they knew what you were planning to do. Are you gonna tell them soon?"

"I'm praying about that, too. It needs to be said at the right time, in the right way—maybe after I pass the GED test."

Gabe stood, feeling the need to end this discussion. "I'd best round up Isaiah so we can get busy on that dog run." He took a few steps toward the door but halted. "Do you know where your daed had planned to build it?"

"He cemented some posts in an area to the left of the barn."

"Okay. You comin' out to keep us company?"

"I've got some things to do inside the house right now, and then there's some corn that needs to be shucked."

"Maybe I'll see you later then." Gabe hurried out of

the barn, grabbed some tools from the back of his buggy, and went to look for Melinda's brother. He hoped a few hours of hard work would get him calmed down.

He found Isaiah digging in the soil just as Melinda had said. Streaks of dirt covered the boy's pale blue shirt and brown trousers, and his face had several dark smudges on it as well.

"What are you doing out here?" Gabe asked, squatting beside Isaiah.

"Lookin' for an old bone Jericho buried some time ago."

Gabe squinted. "What would you be doing that for?"

"My dog's bored and needs somethin' to do. Thought if he had a bone to chew on, he might be happier." Isaiah's mouth turned down at the corners. "Since I'm not supposed to let Jericho off his chain during the day, I figured it wouldn't be good to let him loose in order to look for the bone himself."

"Why not just give him a new bone?"

"Don't have one," Isaiah said with a shrug. "Mama hasn't made any beef soup in a while, and those are the only kind of bones Jericho likes."

Gabe chuckled, already feeling better, and rose to his feet. "How about you and me gettin' busy on that dog run, and you can worry about findin' Jericho a bone later on?"

"Jah, okay." Isaiah stood and slapped the sides of his trousers. Dirt blew everywhere, and Gabe stepped quickly aside.

The boy sneezed, then blew his nose on a dusty hanky he had pulled from his pocket. "You think Jericho will be happier once he has a pen of his own?"

"Maybe so." Gabe clenched his fingers. *I know I'd be happier if I had my own business and was married to Melinda. I've got to figure out some way to make her see how foolish it would be to leave the Amish faith. Doesn't she realize how many people will be hurt if she goes English? Me, most of all.*

Melinda sat on the back porch shucking corn and watching Gabe and Isaiah work under the sweltering sun. She could hear the steady *thump, thump, thump* as they pounded nails to hold the wire fencing that was being connected to the wooden poles Papa Noah had put in.

I wish I could make Gabe understand my need to become a vet. If only he loved me enough to—

A piercing scream halted Melinda's thoughts. Had Gabe been hurt? Was it Isaiah?

She dropped the corn and dashed across the yard.

When Melinda arrived at the dog run, she discovered Isaiah holding his thumb and jumping up and down hollering, "Ouch! Ouch! Oh, that hurts somethin' awful!"

"What happened? Are you seriously injured?"

"He just smacked his thumb with the hammer," Gabe explained. "But he won't let me have a look-see, so I don't know how much damage was done."

"Give me your hand," Melinda ordered, grabbing hold of her brother's arm.

"Don't touch me!"

"I need to see how bad it is."

Isaiah whimpered but finally released his thumb for her inspection.

Melinda held it gently between her fingers. The skin was red and swollen, and the nail was beginning to turn purple. "You might end up losin' that nail," she said with a click of her tongue.

Isaiah sniffed, and a few tears trickled down his cheeks. "How can ya tell? You ain't no doctor."

"No, but she'd like to be," Gabe blurted out.

She glared at him, then looked quickly back at her brother. "What Gabe meant to say is, I've doctored enough animals to know many things. Besides, I lost a couple of nails myself when I slammed two fingers in my bedroom door one time."

Isaiah made no comment. He just stood there rocking back and forth on his heels and moaning.

"You'd best go up to the house and ask Mama to put some ice on your thumb. If it's cared for right away, the nail might not come loose."

"Guess I won't be able to help ya no more, Gabe. Sorry 'bout that," the boy mumbled.

Gabe patted Isaiah on the shoulder. "It's okay. I'll do what I can on my own. We probably wouldn't have gotten it all done today anyway. I'll come back in a few days to finish the project."

"I can help," Melinda volunteered when her brother

scurried away. "After I'm done shucking corn, that is."

Gabe's expression was dubious at first, but then he nodded. "I'll take any help I can get."

fourteen

For the next few weeks, Melinda prayed and searched the Scriptures for answers. She had helped Gabe finish Jericho's dog run, and Gabe had agreed to make Reba a larger cage when he found the time. However, every time she broached the subject of them leaving the Amish faith, they ended up in an argument. Then, before she left for work on Thursday morning, she found a note from Gabe in the birdhouse. He wanted her to go with him to the farmer's market on Saturday after the woodworking shop closed at noon. She had written back, saying she could go and that she wasn't working at the veterinary clinic on this particular Saturday.

Now Melinda sat on the porch swing waiting for him and praying things would go all right between them today. She had to make a decision soon and needed Gabe's final answer as well. Thursday after work she had spoken with Dr. Franklin again, and he'd told her the necessary procedure for getting her GED. So, without her folk's knowledge, she'd gotten the information she needed in order to study for the test and was scheduled to take it at the community college in Springfield in two weeks. Dr. Franklin's wife had agreed to drive her there.

Melinda jumped up when she heard a horse and buggy pull into the yard, figuring it must be Gabe. But as soon as she saw the driver, she realized it was Harold Esh.

"Wie geht's?" the elderly Amish man called as she approached his buggy.

"I'm fine, and you?"

"Can't complain."

"Are you here to see my daed?"

Harold shook his head and stepped down from the buggy. "Found some pheasant eggs in the field this mornin', and their mamm was lyin' dead beside them." He motioned to the cardboard box in the back of his buggy. "Don't believe she'd been gone too long, because the eggs were still warm."

"What do you think happened?"

"Looked like she'd been shot with a pellet gun."

Melinda gasped. "It's not pheasant hunting season yet. I can't understand who would do such a thing."

He shrugged. "Probably some kid usin' the bird for target practice."

Melinda's heart clenched. To think that someone would kill a defenseless animal for the mere sport of it made her feel sick.

"I thought you might like to try and get the eggs to hatch," Harold said.

"I may be able to keep them warm under the heat of a gas lamp, but it would be better if I could get one of our hens to sit on the eggs."

Harold grunted. "I've read about such things but

have never attempted it before."

He reached for the box and handed it to Melinda. "With all the interest you have in animals, you'd probably make a gut vet. 'Course, you'd have to be English for that, I guess."

Melinda's throat constricted. Did Harold know what she was considering? Had Gabe let it slip, or had Dr. Franklin mentioned the idea of her becoming a vet to someone?

"I'm taking some of my pencil drawings into Seymour today," she said, hoping Harold wouldn't pursue the subject. "In the past, I've sold a few pictures to the gift shop at the bed and breakfast there, so I'm hoping they'll want to buy more."

Harold reached under the brim of his straw hat and swiped at the sweat running down his forehead. "Wouldn't think there'd be much money to be made sellin' artwork around these parts."

"The owner of the bed and breakfast told me that lots of tourists who stay there are looking for all kinds of things made by the Amish." Melinda took a step backward. "Well, I'd best get these eggs out to the chicken coop. Thanks for bringing them by, and I'll let you know how it goes."

"Please do." Harold climbed into his buggy and gathered up the reins. "Have a nice time in Seymour, and drive safely."

Melinda hurried off as Harold's buggy rumbled out of the yard. Now if she could only get one of their hens to adopt these eggs.

• • •

Gabe was glad his daed had gone to Springfield this afternoon and decided to close their shop for the rest of the day. That gave him the freedom to take Melinda to the farmer's market without having to ask for time off. Pap was a hard worker and didn't close up any more often than necessary. Whenever Gabe wanted a break from work, Pap usually made some comment like, "Them that works hard eats hearty."

"I work plenty hard," Gabe mumbled as he headed for the house. He planned to grab a couple of molasses cookies, chug down some iced tea, and be on his way to Melinda's.

Inside the kitchen, Gabe found his mother standing in front of their propane-operated stove, where a large enamel kettle sat on the back burner. Steam poured out, and the lid clattered like Pap's old supply wagon when it rumbled down the graveled driveway.

"What are you cookin', Mom?" he asked, washing his hands at the sink.

"I'm canning some beets."

He sniffed deeply of the pungent aroma. "Ah, I wondered if that was what I smelled. Some tasty beets will be real nice come winter."

Gabe went to the refrigerator and retrieved a jug of cold tea, then grabbed a glass from the cupboard and poured himself some. "Sure is hot out there," he remarked.

His mother turned and wiped her damp forehead with the towel that had been lying on the counter.

"And it's even warmer in here." She sighed. "That's the only trouble with canning. It makes the whole kitchen heat up."

Gabe grabbed a cookie from the cookie jar and stuffed it into his mouth. "Umm . . . this is sure gut."

She smiled. "Help yourself to as many as you like. Your sister Karen is coming over tomorrow, and we plan to do some more baking."

He took out six cookies and wrapped them in a paper towel. "Guess I'll eat these on my way over to the Hertzlers' place."

"Going to see Melinda?"

Gabe nodded. "I'm takin' her to the farmer's market in Seymour."

"Sounds like fun. Melinda's a nice girl."

"I think so."

"She and I had a little talk one day when she came by the woodworking shop to see you."

He tipped his head to one side. "Oh? Was it me you were talkin' about?"

Mom chuckled and reached behind the kettle to turn down the burner of the stove. "No. I was asking her advice on how to keep the deer out of my garden."

"What'd she tell you?"

"Suggested a couple of things. One was to put some feed out for the deer along the edge of our property, and it worked." Mom made a sweeping gesture toward her pot of boiling beets. "As you can see, I have plenty of garden produce."

"Melinda's pretty smart when it comes to things like

that." *She just ain't so smart when it comes to making a decision that would affect the rest of her life.* He glanced at his mother. *Sure wish I could talk this over with Mom. She's always full of good advice and might have some idea how I can get Melinda to see things from my point of view.*

"Are you troubled about something, son?" his mother asked. "You look a bit *umgerennt.*"

Gabe shook his head. "I ain't upset. Just feelin' confused about some things."

"Want to talk about it?"

Of course he wanted to talk about it, but Gabe thought about his promise to Melinda not to mention her plans to anyone, and he couldn't go back on his word. "Naw, I'll figure things out in due time."

Mom smiled. "I'm sure you will. Now run along and have yourself a gut day at the market."

"I will." Gabe headed out the door.

A short time later, he was headed toward the Hertzlers' place. As he gave his horse the freedom to trot, he thought about Melinda and prayed she would change her mind about becoming a vet. He had been reading his Bible every night and asking God to show him if leaving the Amish faith was the right thing for either of them to do. So far, he'd felt no direction other than to keep working toward his goal of opening his own woodworking shop. If only Melinda would be content to marry him and stay in Webster County as an Amish woman who only looked after needy animals, the way she was doing now. It didn't seem right that she would want to follow in her mother's footsteps and leave the Amish faith to pursue a strictly English career.

When Gabe finally pulled into the Hertzlers' driveway, he was all worked up. What he really wanted to do was tell Melinda exactly how he felt about things, but he didn't want to spoil their day at the farmer's market by initiating another argument. So, with a firm resolve to hold his tongue, he hopped out of his buggy and secured the horse to the hitching rail. He glanced up at the house, hoping Melinda would be on the porch waiting for him, but no one was in sight. He scanned the yard, but the only thing moving was Isaiah's dog, pacing back and forth in his new pen.

Gabe meandered over to see Jericho, and the mutt wagged his tail and barked a friendly greeting.

"You like your pen, boy?" Gabe reached through the wire, gave the dog a quick pat on the head, and then headed for the house. He was almost to the back door when he heard the sound of yodeling coming from the chicken coop.

"That has to be Melinda," he said with a chuckle.

He strode toward the coop and found Melinda on her knees in front of some eggs that were nestled in a wooden box filled with straw.

"What are you doing?" Gabe asked, shutting the door behind him.

Melinda lifted her head and smiled. "I'm watching to see if one of our hens will sit on some pheasant eggs Harold Esh brought by awhile ago."

Gabe squatted beside her. "How come?"

"The mother pheasant had been killed, and since the eggs were still warm, Harold thought I might be able to get them to hatch."

Gabe shook his head. "You may as well become a vet, because everyone in Webster County thinks they should bring their ailing, orphaned, or crippled animals to you."

Melinda looked at him pointedly. "You really think so?"

Gabe could have bit his tongue. Of course he didn't think she should become a vet. "It was just a figure of speech," he mumbled.

"I really do like caring for animals," she said wistfully.

"I know."

"And you're still praying about it?"

He nodded.

"Any idea how long it will be before you give me your answer?"

He shrugged. "Can't really say. Gotta be clear about things before I can make such a life-changing decision."

"Okay. I'll try not to mention it the rest of the day." Melinda pointed to the pheasant eggs lying in the nest of straw. "I wonder how I can coax one of the chickens to sit on these."

In one quick motion, Gabe reached out, grabbed a fat red hen, and plunked her on top of the eggs. He didn't know who was the most surprised when the chicken stayed put, him or Melinda.

"She's accepting them!" Melinda clapped her hands. "Oh, Gabe, you're a genius. I should have thought to do that."

Gabe smiled and took Melinda's hand as they both stood. "Ready to go to Seymour?"

She nodded toward the hen. "I'd better wait and see how things go. She might decide not to stay on the nest."

Gabe's face heated as irritation set in. "You'd give up an afternoon at the market to stay home and babysit a bunch of pheasant eggs?"

She shrugged.

"If your animals are more important than me, then I guess I'll head to Seymour alone."

Melinda's eyes were filled with tears. "Please don't be mad."

Gabe hated it when she cried, and he pulled her quickly into his arms. "I'm not mad, just hurt because you'd rather be out in the chicken coop than spend the afternoon with me."

"That's not true." Her voice shook with emotion. "I do want to go to the farmer's market with you today."

He glanced at the setting hen. "Does that mean you'll go then?"

She nodded. "Jah, okay. It looks like the eggs will be all right. I'll check on them again after we get back."

Gabe lowered his head and kissed her. The kiss was the only good thing that had come from their little disagreement, but it didn't solve their biggest problem—that of Melinda wanting to leave home. If only there was an easy solution.

fifteen

When they pulled into the parking lot at the farmer's market, Melinda felt a sense of excitement. She had always enjoyed coming here and remembered several times when she was a little girl and had spent the day with her mamm. She thought about one time when she and Mama met Papa Noah at the farmer's market, before they were a couple. After leaving the market, the three of them had gone to lunch at the Hillbilly Café, and Melinda had enjoyed Mama's jokes and listening to country music.

"Maybe we can eat at the Hillbilly Café today," she suggested.

"Or how about Don's Pizza Place?"

"That might be better," she agreed. "It's closer to the farmer's market and isn't too far from the bed and breakfast where they sell Grandpa's rhubarb-strawberry jam and some of my drawings."

Gabe jumped down to help Melinda out of the buggy. "We can have lunch wherever you want."

Melinda smiled.

"So where shall we start first?" Gabe asked as they walked toward the booths on the other side of the parking lot.

"Wherever you like."

He took her hand and gave it a gentle squeeze. "I like it when we're not arguing."

"Me, too."

They walked hand in hand until they came to a booth where an English man was selling wooden holders for trash cans. They resembled a small cupboard, but the door opened from the top, and the trash can was placed inside.

Gabe seemed to be quite impressed and asked the man several questions. They soon learned that he lived up north near Kansas City and had been heading to Branson to sell some of his wooden items to a gift shop there. He had heard about the farmer's market in Seymour and decided to rent a booth and sell some of his things.

"I think I could make something like that and probably sell 'em for a lot less money than his are goin' for," Gabe whispered to Melinda as they moved to another booth. "In fact, I believe I'll make one to give Mom for Christmas this year."

"Have you ever thought you could make and sell wooden items if you lived in the English world?" Melinda blurted without thinking.

Gabe frowned, and she knew she had spoiled their wonderful day together.

Melinda lounged on a log in the woods behind their home, where she had been sitting for the last several minutes, sketching two does eating some corn she'd scattered on the ground.

She thought about the way Gabe looked at her when he'd brought her home from the farmer's market earlier today—like he wanted to clear the air but was afraid to say anything for fear they would have another disagreement. So instead of talking things out, Gabe had said good-bye without even giving her a kiss. And when she had invited him to stay for supper, he'd turned her down, saying he had somewhere else to go this evening.

"We can't continue on like this much longer," Melinda murmured. "We both need to make a decision soon."

She glanced back at the deer grazing a few feet away. They looked so peaceful she almost envied them.

"You're too pretty for anyone to kill," she whispered.

Pow! Pow! Pow!

Melinda jumped at the sound of a gun being fired, and the deer scattered.

"*Was is letz do*—what is wrong here? It's not hunting season yet." She dropped her tablet and pencil into the canvas tote at her feet, slung it over her shoulder, and followed the repeated popping sounds.

As Melinda stepped into an open field, the sight that greeted her sent a shock wave spiraling from the top of her head all the way to her toes. There stood Gabe, holding a gun, as he fired continuously at a target nailed to a tree several yards away.

Melinda remained motionless, unable to think, speak, or even breathe. Gabe kept on shooting, apparently unaware of her presence. When he ran out of bullets and began to reload, she marched up to him and poked her finger in his back. "Just what do you think you're doing?"

He whirled around. "Melinda, you scared me half to death."

"And thanks to that noisy gun of yours, you scared the deer away that I had been sketching." Melinda's voice trembled, and her ears tingled.

"Sorry about that, but I'm target practicing—getting ready for fall, when hunting season opens." Gabe's eyebrows squeezed together. As he stared at her, the silence between them was thick like cream, only not nearly as pleasant. "If I'd known you were nearby trying to draw a picture, I wouldn't have shot the gun."

Melinda's hands shook as she held them at her sides. "So this is where you planned to come after you dropped me off, huh?"

"Jah."

"Why didn't you just tell me that you had planned to target practice?"

His chest expanded with a deep breath, then fell when he exhaled. "I didn't think you'd want to hear it."

"How come?"

"I know how you feel about hunting, Melinda. I figured we'd end up having another argument."

Melinda planted both hands on her hips and stared at him. "The creatures in these woods are dear to me."

"And I'm not?" Gabe's eyelids fluttered in rapid succession. "Do the deer mean more to you than me?"

Melinda stared at the toes of her sneakers. How could she make him understand?

"I do love you, Gabe, but I care about the animals God created, too. That's why I want to become a—"

"God made many animals for us to eat—deer included," Gabe said, cutting Melinda off. "In the ninth chapter of Genesis, God told Noah that 'every moving thing that liveth, shall be meat for you.' "

"Jah, well," Melinda huffed, "I'd better not see you on my folks' property with your gun again. I'm going home right now and ask Papa Noah to post NO HUNTING signs on our land."

Gabe's mouth dropped open. "You're kidding!"

"I'm not."

"Listen, Melinda, you can't save every deer in the woods."

"I know that, but I can save those in *our* woods."

Gabe's only response was a disgruntled groan.

"And since we're already arguing—I think it's time we both make a decision."

"A decision?"

She nodded. "About me becoming a veterinarian and us leaving the Amish faith."

"I can't leave, Melinda."

"Can't or won't?"

He stared at the ground. "I love you, but—"

"But not enough to help me realize my dream?"

"I—I want you to be happy, but I don't think leaving family and friends to become a vet will bring you the happiness you're looking for."

"This isn't about happiness, Gabe." She squeezed her eyes shut. "It's about helping animals—as many as I can."

"I think you're obsessed with the whole idea, and I

don't believe you've thought it all through."

Melinda opened her eyes. "For several weeks I've done nothing but think and pray about this. I had thought that if you were in agreement with me and were willing to start a new life in the English world, I would know it was God's will."

"But I'm not willing, so it must not be God's will. Can't you see that?"

She shook her head. "You're confusing me."

He reached his hand out to her, but she backed away. "I—I need to go."

"Please don't, Melinda. Stay, and let's talk about this some more."

She turned her hands palm up. "What else is there to say? You want to stay Amish, and I want to—no, need to—leave the faith."

"But you don't need to. You can—"

Melinda pivoted away from Gabe before he could finish his sentence. Clutching tightly to the canvas bag slung over her shoulder, she fled for home.

sixteen

As Gabe watched Melinda run away from him, he wondered how the day could have ended on such a sour note. There had to be some way to make Melinda aware of how much he loved her. And if she realized it, she might change her mind about leaving the Amish faith.

Gabe dropped to a seat on a nearby log and stared at his gun. *If I gave up hunting, would that make her happy?* He shook his head. *No, that's not our main problem. Even if I were to promise never to hunt another deer, I think she would still want to leave home and become a vet.*

He sat there several seconds, pondering things and praying for guidance, until an idea popped into his head. He jumped up. "I'm going home right now and make Melinda a special gift—something that will let her know how much I care. Something she can't take to any old college."

Melinda had just stepped into the yard when she spotted Susie climbing down from her buggy.

"Have you been in the woods again?" Susie asked as Melinda drew near.

"Jah. I was drawing a picture of some deer. Until Gabe scared them off, that is."

Susie's forehead wrinkled. "How'd he do that?"

"He had a gun and was shooting at a target nailed to a tree."

"You'd better get used to hearing guns go off," Susie said. "Soon it will be hunting season."

"It's not me I'm worried about. My concern is for the deer."

"Many of our men hunt," Susie reminded her. "It's just the way of things."

"I know, and I realize I can't save every deer in the woods. I can protect those who come onto our property, though."

"So if you know that, then don't be so hard on Gabe."

Susie gave Melinda a hug. "I'm sure he loves you."

"Then he should prove it."

"I think he did when he asked you to marry him."

Melinda's mouth fell open. "You know about that?"

Susie nodded. "Heard it from Gabe's mamm when I was working at Kaulp's Store last week. She dropped by to get—"

"Gabe must have told her," Melinda interrupted with a shake of her head. "I can't believe he'd do that after we agreed to keep it quiet until we had set a date."

"I don't see what the big secret is." Susie leaned against the buggy and folded her arms.

"Things seem to be going from bad to worse between Gabe and me." Melinda drew in a shaky breath. "I'm beginning to wonder if I made a mistake in agreeing to marry him."

Susie shook her head. "You can't mean that. I think you're just upset about Gabe hunting and you're not thinking straight."

"You're right, I am upset, but there's more involved than just him wanting to hunt. More than you realize, Susie." Tears trickled down Melinda's cheeks, and she swiped at them with the back of her hand.

"I realize this—if Gabe were my boyfriend, I'd do everything I could to make him happy. He's a gut man and would make a fine husband."

"I know he's a good man, but he doesn't love me enough to—" Melinda's voice trailed off, and she looked away.

"To what?"

"To—to leave the Amish faith with me." Melinda choked on her final words.

"What? Please tell me you're kidding."

Melinda shook her head.

Susie grabbed Melinda's arm and pulled her toward the buggy. "Let's have a seat and you can tell me about this crazy notion."

For the next several minutes, Melinda sat beside Susie on the front seat of her buggy as she told about Dr. Franklin's suggestion that she become a vet. She also explained that she planned to take her GED and gave a detailed account of Gabe's reaction to it all.

"He said he would pray about things, but then we had an argument in the woods over him target practicing so he can hunt in the fall, and he ended up telling me that he won't leave the Amish faith."

Susie just sat there shaking her head and mumbling over and over, "I can't believe this. I just can't believe it."

"You think I'm wrong for wanting to take care of animals, too, don't you?" Melinda asked, giving her aunt a little nudge with her elbow.

"Not wrong for wanting to care for animals. Just wrong for wanting to leave the only life you've ever known."

"That's not true," Melinda corrected. "I lived in the English world with my mamm and my real daed until I was six years old."

"*Puh!* You can't tell me you remember much about that."

"No, I guess not, but I do remember some things, and I—"

Susie groaned. "I can't even imagine how it would be not to have you in my life, Melinda. Don't you know if you leave the faith, we'll have to shun you?"

"Jah, I know."

"There's nothin' in this whole world that would make me want to move away from my family and friends. Not even love or money."

Melinda nibbled on the inside of her cheek. "This hasn't been an easy decision for me, Susie. I know the sacrifices I would have to make, but I feel a strong need to care for animals, and I can't do it properly unless I have professional training."

"What do your folks say about all this?" Susie asked.

"They don't know yet."

Susie's eyebrows lifted, and her eyes became huge. "You haven't told 'em?"

Melinda shook her head.

"Not even that Gabe has asked you to marry him?"

"No. I was waiting until after I passed my GED test to tell them what I'm thinking of doing, and since Gabe's not going to leave the Amish faith, there's really no point in telling them about his marriage proposal, now is there?"

Susie shrugged. "I guess not."

Melinda clasped Susie's hand. "You've got to promise me you won't say a word about this to anyone. Do I have your word?"

"It won't be easy, but jah, I'll keep quiet about it."

● ● ●

On Monday morning, Melinda stopped at the bird-house out front before she headed for work. She discovered a note from Gabe.

Dear Melinda,

I'm really sorry about our disagreement yesterday, and I hope we can resolve all our differences. I was wondering if you would be free to go on a picnic supper with me this evening. I will bring the food, and I'll check the birdhouse for an answer before I pick you up. If you're willing, we can leave around six o'clock.

Always yours,
Gabe

Melinda smiled. *Gabe said he was sorry. Does that mean he's changed his mind about staying Amish?*

She removed the pencil and tablet from the birdhouse and scrawled a note in return.

Dear Gabe,

I accept your apology, and I hope we can settle things between us. A picnic supper sounds nice. I'll be waiting for you at six, and I'll bring a loaf of homemade bread and some of Grandpa's rhubarb-strawberry jam.

Yours fawnly,
Melinda

With a feeling of anticipation, she slipped the note into the birdhouse and climbed back into her buggy.

"Melinda, can you come here a minute?" Dr. Franklin called from examining room one.

Melinda set her mop aside and entered the room. "What do you need, Dr. Franklin?"

"Would you mind holding Sparky while I cut his toenails?"

"Sure, I'd be happy to help." Melinda stood on the left side of the examining table and held the little Scottie dog around the middle with one hand. With her other hand she held his front paw so the doctor's hands were free to do the clipping. She'd assisted him several times when he had a dog's nails to trim, and the animals always seemed relaxed and calm in her presence.

"Say, Dr. Franklin, I've been wondering about something . . ."

"What's that, Melinda?"

"Well, actually, it's more Isaiah who's wanting to know the answer to a question."

He glanced up at her. "What does your little brother want to know?"

"Well, Isaiah told me one day that he'd heard that if a dog has a dark mouth it means he's smart. But if the inside of his mouth is light, then he'll likely be dumb." She giggled, feeling kind of self-conscious for having asked such a silly question. "I told him it was probably just an old wives' tale, but he said I should ask you about it."

The doctor continued to clip Sparky's nails. "Actually, there's some truth in what young Isaiah told you. It's not documented that I know of, but many animal breeders take stock in the color of a dog's mouth, and I've heard it said that a dark mouth means a smart dog."

"Hmm . . . that's interesting."

"Sparky's sure doing well," Dr. Franklin commented. "He's a lot more relaxed with you holding him than he ever is when I try working on him alone."

Melinda just smiled in response. It made her feel good to be helping the doctor, and if she could help an animal relax, it was an added bonus.

"If you were a certified vet's assistant, I'd have you helping with many other things here in the clinic," the doctor said with a smile.

"Jah, I know."

"And if you ever do become a veterinarian, I might consider taking you on as a partner some day."

"Really?" Melinda's heart swelled with joy. How wonderful it would be to work side by side with Dr. Franklin as his partner, not just someone who cleaned up the clinic, helped with toenail clipping, or gave a flea bath now and then.

"Yes, I really mean it. In fact, I've been thinking that I'd like to help with your schooling."

"Help?"

"Yes. Financially."

Her mouth fell open. "You would really do that for me?"

He nodded. "As you know, my wife and I have no children of our own. So it would give me pleasure to help someone who has such a special way with animals. You've got potential, Melinda, and I would like to see you use your talents to the best of your abilities."

"And you think in order to do that I'd need to go to school and become a vet?"

The doctor nodded. "I don't want to influence you one way or the other, but if you were my daughter, I would do everything in my power to make it happen." He set the clippers aside. "There you go, Sparky. All done until next time."

"Want me to put him in one of the cages in the back room until his owner comes to pick him up?" Melinda asked.

"Yes, if you don't mind."

"Don't mind a'tall." She scooped the terrier into her arms and started for the door.

"Oh, Melinda . . . one more thing," Dr. Franklin called. She turned back around.

"I know my wife said she would drive you to Springfield next Friday to take your GED test, but her mother, who lives in Mansfield, fell and broke her hip last week. So Marcia will be helping her for the next couple of weeks."

Melinda forced a smile. "That's all right. I'm sure I can find someone else to drive me that day. I'll also need to give my folks a legitimate reason for me going to Springfield by myself."

"And you're still planning to wait and tell them after you've taken the test?" he asked.

"Jah. I mean, yes."

He smiled. "Well, I hope it all works out for you."

"Me, too, Dr. Franklin."

seventeen

When Melinda returned home from the veterinary clinic later that day, she found her mother at the kitchen sink, peeling potatoes.

"How was your day?" Mama asked over her shoulder.

"It was gut. Dr. Franklin had me hold a terrier so he could clip its nails. He said the animal seemed calmer with me there."

"Will you keep working at the vet's after you and Gabe are married?"

Melinda sank to a seat at the table. "Who told you Gabe had asked me to marry him?"

"Heard it from Freda Kaulp when I went to her store earlier today. She overheard Susie and Leah Swartz's conversation the other day." Mama sounded disappointed, and Melinda knew it wasn't that she didn't want Melinda to marry Gabe. More than likely, her mamm was hurt because Melinda hadn't told her the news herself.

"I'm sorry you had to hear it secondhand," Melinda apologized. "When Gabe proposed, we decided not to tell anyone until we had set a date." She sighed.

"Guess Gabe must have told his mother, though. How else would Freda have found out?"

Mama washed and dried her hands, then joined Melinda at the table. "So, have the two of you set a wedding date?"

Melinda shook her head. "Not yet. We've had a couple of disagreements lately, and I don't want to make any definite plans until we get some things resolved." Oh, how she hated keeping secrets from her mamm. It would feel so good to tell the whole story about her wanting to become a vet and Gabe being unwilling to leave the Amish faith with her. *But Mama would be upset if she knew I was thinking of leaving, and until I know for sure what I'm going to do, I don't see any point in upsetting her.*

Mama reached over and took Melinda's hand. "We're all human, and disagreements come up, even between two people in love."

Melinda's only response was a quick nod.

"Just keep God in the center of your lives, live each day to the fullest, and after you're married, never go to bed angry at one another." Mama smiled. "It's important to work through your differences and pray about things rather than harboring resentment if you don't always get your way."

"I know that, Mama, but it's not always as easy as it seems." Melinda fiddled with the stack of paper napkins piled in a small basket on the table. "Gabe's coming by around six o'clock to take me on a picnic supper, so maybe we can talk some things through then."

"That sounds nice. Will you want help filling the picnic basket?"

"The note he left me in the birdhouse out front said he's going to furnish the food, but I thought it might be nice if I took a loaf of bread and some of Grandpa's good-tasting jam."

"I baked a batch of honey wheat bread this morning, so help yourself to a loaf. And there's several pints of Grandpa's rhubarb-strawberry jam in the pantry." Her mother popped a couple of her knuckles and smiled.

Melinda cringed. "Doesn't it hurt when you do that?"

"To me it feels good. Helps my fingers not get so stiff."

Melinda shrugged. She didn't think she would ever want to crack her knuckles, no matter how old she was or how stiff her fingers might become. She pushed away from the table and stood. "Guess I'd better get my cat's supper ready before I go upstairs to change clothes for my picnic date with Gabe." She cupped her hands around her mouth and called, "Here Snow! Come, kitty, kitty. It's time for your dinner."

"That's odd," Melinda said when her cat didn't show herself. "Snow usually comes running on the first call. Have you seen her, Mama?"

"Not since early this morning when she was racing around the house like her tail was on fire. I figured she might be after a mouse or something."

"Has she been outside today?"

"Not that I know of." Mama clicked her tongue.

"I've never known a cat that liked to hang around the house the way that one does."

Melinda frowned. "You don't suppose Isaiah's playing a trick on me and has hidden her someplace?"

"He's upstairs in his room. Why don't you go ask him?"

"I think I will." Melinda started for the stairs.

"I hope you find Snow. I know how much you care for that cat," her mother called.

"Jah, I care about all my animals." Melinda sprinted up the stairs, making her first stop Isaiah's bedroom, where she knocked on the door.

"Come in!"

She found her brother sprawled on the bed with a book in his hands. "Have you seen Snow?"

"Not since last winter. Sure hope we get plenty this year, 'cause I plan to do some sledding."

Melinda shook her head. "Ha! You must get your funny bone from our mamm."

"Jah, Mama can be kind of silly at times."

"Now, seriously, have you seen my cat today?"

Isaiah closed his book and sat up. "No, but awhile ago I thought I heard her out in the hall."

"Upstairs or down?"

"Up here."

"You heard Snow but didn't see her?"

"Right. Heard her meowing, and then it stopped. I figured she'd gone downstairs."

Feeling as though she might be getting a headache, Melinda made little circles with her fingertips along

142

the side of her forehead. "I didn't see any sign of Snow downstairs, and when I called, she didn't come. It's not like her to hide when it's time to eat."

"Maybe she ain't hungry."

"Always has been before." Melinda leaned against the door jam. "Has she been in the house all day?"

"Don't know. Haven't seen her at all."

Meow. Meow.

Melinda cocked her head. "Did you hear that?"

"Yep. Sounds like Snow's somewhere nearby."

"I'm going to find her." Melinda left the room and followed the meowing sounds until she came to a small hole in the linen closet at the end of the hallway. It seemed too little for her cat to have gone through, yet she could hear Snow's pathetic meows inside the wall.

The first thing Gabe did when he pulled into the Hertzlers' driveway was to check the birdhouse to see if there was a response from Melinda. Sure enough, she had left a note saying she would go on the picnic supper with him.

He grinned and glanced at the surprise he had in the back of his buggy. He hoped she would be so pleased with the gift that she would see how much he loved her and change her mind about leaving home.

Gabe hopped back into the buggy and picked up the reins. A few minutes later, he tied his horse to the hitching rail and took the porch steps two at a time. He rapped on the door and waited. It took awhile for someone to answer, and when the door finally opened, it was Melinda's brother who stood on the other side.

"I came by to pick up Melinda. Is she ready?"

Isaiah shook his head. "Don't think so. She's sittin' in front of a hole in the wall upstairs."

Gabe's eyebrows lifted. "Why would she be doing that?"

"Her cat's stuck there, and she can't figure out how to get the silly critter out. The hole's too small for her to reach her hand into."

"What does your daed have to say? Can't he cut a bigger hole?"

Isaiah shrugged. "Guess he could, but Papa ain't here. He's workin' late at the tree farm and probably won't be home 'til almost dark."

"Think I'd better see what I can do to help," Gabe said, stepping into the house.

Isaiah led the way, and Gabe followed him up the stairs and down the hall until they came to the linen closet where Melinda and her mother were on their knees calling to the kitten.

Gabe cleared his throat, and Melinda looked up at him. "Snow seems to have squeezed through this tiny hole, but she can't get back out."

"She was probably after a mouse," Faith put in.

"I can cut a bigger hole if you want me to," Gabe offered. "Where's Noah keep his saws?"

"Out in the barn," Faith replied. "Isaiah, run out there and get one of your daed's saws."

The boy scampered off, and Gabe squatted beside

144

Melinda. "I can patch the hole I make with a piece of Sheetrock, and it'll be good as new."

"What if Snow won't come to me once the hole is bigger?" Melinda asked.

Meow! Meow!

"Does that answer your question?" Gabe smiled. "Sounds like your cat can't wait to get out."

"I agree," Faith said. "Once Gabe cuts a bigger hole, you can stick your hand inside. I'm sure Snow will come right away."

Isaiah showed up a few minutes later, holding a small handsaw, which he handed to Gabe. It didn't take long for Gabe to make a larger opening, and he was careful not to let the blade of the saw stick too far through the other side. If he cut the cat by mistake, Melinda would never forgive him, and it would be just one more reason for her to leave home.

Once the opening was made and the Sheetrock removed, Melinda put her hand inside. "Here, Snow. Come, kitty, kitty"

There was a faint *meow,* and when Melinda pulled her hand out again, she had Snow by the nape of the neck. Gabe breathed a sigh of relief. The cat was okay.

"Danki, Gabe." Tears pooled in Melinda's eyes.

"You're welcome." *Maybe now she'll realize how much she needs me.*

"I think I'll take Snow downstairs and feed her while Gabe patches the hole." Melinda stood and hurried from the room.

"If there's a scrap of Sheetrock in the barn I can fix

the hole now," Gabe said to Faith. "If not, I'll bring some over later on."

Half an hour later, he and Melinda stood in front of his open buggy. He had patched the hole with a piece of plywood he'd found in the barn and would come back tomorrow with Sheetrock, tape, and the mud to do the job correctly.

"See that piece of canvas I have in my buggy?" Gabe said, motioning to the back.

Melinda nodded.

"Pull it aside and take a look at what I made for you last night."

"Is it a trash can holder like the one we saw at the farmer's market?"

He shook his head. "It's something I hope you'll like even better."

Melinda gave the canvas a quick yank, and when a long wooden object came into view, she tipped her head in question. "What is this?"

"It's a feeding trough," he explained. "To feed the deer in your woods."

"And if they come to our place to eat, they'll be safe from hunters." Melinda threw herself into Gabe's arms and squeezed him around the neck. "I'm glad you want to care for the deer now rather than kill them."

Gabe swallowed hard. How could he admit to Melinda that he had no intention of giving up hunting? He just wouldn't be doing it on her folks' land.

eighteen

With the warm August breeze tickling her nose, Melinda leaned back on her elbows and sighed. Gabe's picnic supper of barbecued beef sandwiches, dill pickles, and potato salad left her feeling full and satisfied. Even though he admitted that his mother had made most of the meal, Melinda appreciated the gesture. Gabe seemed to enjoy Mama's homemade bread, too, for he ate several pieces of it slathered with Grandpa's jam.

Careful not to ruin their picnic, Melinda hadn't asked Gabe yet if he'd told his mother that he had proposed. She thought it would be best to wait awhile on that. So, they'd only had a pleasant chat on the drive from her house over to the pond, and for the last hour, they had been sitting on an old quilt enjoying the picnic supper and having more lighthearted conversation.

Melinda glanced over at Gabe. His eyes were closed, and his face was lifted toward the sky. *If I can't get him to change his mind about going English, and I have to go out on my own, I'll surely miss him. It doesn't seem fair that I'm expected to choose between those I love and the joy of caring for animals.*

As if sensing her watching him, Gabe opened his eyes.

"Were you sleeping?" she asked.

He smiled at her in such a sweet way, it sent shivers up her spine. "Just enjoyin' the sun and thinkin' about how much I want to make you my wife."

Her cheeks warmed. "Gabe—I—"

"Whatever differences we may have, can't we just agree to disagree?"

There was a little crease in the middle of Gabe's forehead, and Melinda reached up to rub it away. "I wish it was that simple."

"You love me, and I love you. We shouldn't allow anything to come between us."

Melinda started to reply, but Gabe stopped her with a kiss so pleasant it took her breath away. She couldn't think when she was in his arms. At this moment, nothing mattered except the two of them sharing a special time of being alone together.

"Let's go for a walk," he said suddenly. "When we get back we can have some of that apple crisp Mom made for our dessert."

Melinda nodded, and he helped her to her feet. As they walked together among the pine trees, she knew these wonderful moments she'd shared with Gabe would stay forever locked in her brain.

"I hate to spoil the evening," Gabe said, "but there are some things we need to discuss."

"You're right, there are," she agreed. "And I also have a question I want to ask you."

"Go ahead. You can ask me anything, Melinda."

"Did you tell your mamm that you had asked me to marry you?"

Gabe stopped walking, and so did she. "I hope you don't mind, but Mom came right out and asked how serious I was about you. So I felt she had the right to know that I'd proposed marriage."

"I see. Well, apparently, your mamm told Susie when she dropped by Kaulp's General Store, and Freda Kaulp overheard the conversation and then told my mamm today."

Gabe's forehead wrinkled. "I'm sorry she had to hear it that way, but you really should have told your folks yourself, Melinda. Don't you agree?"

Melinda was thinking of her response when she heard a noise. "Did you hear that?"

He shrugged. "Didn't hear anything except the rustle of leaves when the wind picked up."

"Listen, there it is again—a strange thrashing sound." Melinda let go of Gabe's hand and hurried off.

"Where are you going?" he called.

"To see what that noise is."

"Not without me, you're not. It might be some wild animal."

When they came upon the source of the noise, Melinda was shocked to discover a young doe with its leg caught in a metal trap. The poor animal thrashed about, obviously trying to free itself.

"Oh no!" She rushed toward the deer, but Gabe grabbed her around the waist and held her steady.

"What are you tryin' to do, get yourself hurt?"

"I need to free the deer and make sure her leg's not broken."

"Melinda, I don't think that's such a good idea."

She wiggled free and went down on her knees.

• • •

Gabe watched as Melinda crawled slowly toward the deer. He didn't like her taking chances like this but figured if he made an issue of it, she would get mad. *All I want is to keep her safe—locked in my heart and loved forever.*

The doe lay on its belly with the trapped foot extended in front of her. It stopped thrashing and twitched its ears when Melinda approached. It was almost as if the critter knew she was there to help.

Wish there was something I could do, but if I got as close to the deer as Melinda is, it would most likely spook. Animals aren't as comfortable around me as they seem to be with her. Gabe held his breath as Melinda pressed the sides of the trap apart, freeing the animal's leg. An instant later, the deer jumped up and bolted into a thicket of tall shrubs.

"I wish I'd had the chance to check it over," Melinda said when she returned to his side. "I'm sure the doe's leg must have been cut." She shook her head. "I'll never understand why anyone would want to hurt a beautiful deer like that."

Gabe resisted the temptation to argue that hunting deer for food was perfectly acceptable to his way of thinking. But he knew they would argue if he broached that subject again. Besides, setting a trap was no way to catch a deer, or any other animal, as far as he was concerned. And to make matters worse, it wasn't even hunting season yet.

Gabe checked the trap to be sure it would no

longer work, and then he buried it in the dirt.

"See why I asked Papa Noah to post No Hunting signs on our property?" Melinda's eyes shimmered with tears.

"Let's head back to our picnic spot and eat our dessert," he said, rather than comment on her last statement.

She shook her head. "No thanks. I have no appetite for food right now."

Melinda and Gabe had only gone a few feet when she spotted a baby skunk scampering out of the bushes. "Oh, look, Gabe! Isn't it cute? I wonder if it's an orphan."

"Don't get any dumb ideas, Melinda."

She halted and held her breath, waiting to see what the little skunk would do next. If it wasn't orphaned, she was sure its mother would show up soon.

"Melinda, let's go."

She shook her head. "I need to see if the skunk's mother is around."

"If she does come on the scene, we could be in a lot of trouble." Gabe grabbed Melinda's hand and gave it a tug, but she pulled it away.

"I'm not going back until I know the baby's not alone."

"And if it is?"

"I'll take it back to my place so I can care for it."

"No way! I won't allow no skunk in my buggy. What if it sprays?"

"Baby skunks never spray unless they're bothered, Gabe."

"Jah, well, pickin' up a skunk and haulin' it home in a buggy could easily be considered 'bothering.'"

Melinda tiptoed a bit closer to the small creature, but she had only taken a few steps when the baby's mother trotted out of the bushes. Before Melinda had the presence of mind to turn and run, the skunk lifted its tail and let loose with a disgusting spray.

"Let's get out of here!" Gabe hollered.

Melinda and Gabe raced toward his buggy. They were about to climb in when he stopped her.

"What's wrong?"

"It's bad enough that we both smell like a skunk. If we get into my buggy, it'll stink, too."

She clicked her tongue. "We can't walk home. It's too far."

"You're right, but my buggy will never be the same after this trip to the woods."

Melinda hung her head. "I'm sorry. It was my fault. I just wanted to be sure the skunk wasn't orphaned, and—" She stopped talking when her eyes started to water.

"Don't cry, Melinda. I hate it when you cry."

"I'm not crying. My eyes are watering because of this awful odor." She fanned her face and whirled around a few times. "Phew! Did you ever smell anything so awful?"

Gabe shook his head. "Not since we found a batch of rotten eggs out behind our house." He plugged his nose.

"And even that didn't smell half as bad as we do now."

"I'll help you wash down the buggy," she promised.

"We've got to get this smell off ourselves first."

She nodded. "I know. Maybe Dr. Franklin has something we can use to get the odor out of the buggy."

"My dog Shep got himself mixed up with a skunk once," Gabe said. "We bathed him in tomato juice."

"Did it help?"

"Some, but it took weeks before that animal smelled like a dog again."

Melinda folded her arms. "That's not exactly what I wanted to hear."

Gabe laughed, and so did she. At least it had only been a skunk that had come between them this time. And they'd been able to find some humor in it. That was a good sign that things were improving in their relationship. At any rate, she hoped they were.

nineteen

Melinda awoke on Friday morning with a sense of excitement. Today she would be going to Springfield to take her GED test at the community college. Their English neighbor Ellen Watts had agreed to give her a ride, but Melinda had only told her folks that she was going to Springfield to do some shopping today. It was true. She was planning to shop for a few things at the discount store there after she had taken her test.

Melinda hurried to wash and get dressed, and then

headed for the kitchen to help her mother with breakfast. Usually Mama was already up and scurrying about, but today she found the kitchen empty.

"Where's Mama?" she asked Papa Noah when he came in from doing his morning chores a short time later. "Was she outside with you?"

He shook his head. "Your mamm's come down with the flu. Woke up with it during the night."

Melinda felt immediate concern. "I'm sorry to hear that. Is there anything I can do?"

"I'd appreciate it if you would cancel your shopping trip in Springfield today," he said, hanging his straw hat on a wall peg by the door. "She can't keep anything down and is as weak as a kitten. I don't think it's a good idea for her to be here alone."

"What about Isaiah? Won't he be home today?"

Papa Noah shook his head. "Hank Osborn is shorthanded, with a couple of fellows also out with the flu, so I'm takin' Isaiah to help at the tree farm today."

She nibbled on the inside of her cheek. "How about Grandpa? Can't he keep an eye out for Mama today?"

"He's got his own share of health problems, Melinda, and I don't think it's a good idea for him to be exposed to your mamm when she's sick, do you?"

"No, of course not." Melinda sighed. "You're right, Papa Noah. I should be the one to care for Mama today. I'll run over to Ellen Watts's house and tell her I won't be needing a ride to Springfield today after all."

Papa Noah smiled. "Danki. You're a helpful

daughter, and I can go to work today with the peace of mind that my wife will be in gut hands."

Melinda reached for her choring apron, also hanging on a wall peg. *Guess I'll have to wait a few more weeks to take that test. Maybe by then I'll be even more prepared.*

Gabe stood in front of his workbench sanding the arms of a wooden rocking chair. It was a nice change from working on cabinets, which was what Pap usually stuck him with. However, he would rather have been working on the gun stock he'd promised to make for Aaron. After his friend saw how nice Gabe's stock had turned out, he'd placed an order for one just like it. A couple other men in their community had also asked Gabe to make them a new gun stock, which meant he had plenty of his own work to keep him busy after regular working hours.

If I keep getting orders for gun stocks, I might be able to open my own business sooner than I expected. If I had my own place, Melinda might realize why I don't want to leave our community and start life over in the English world.

Gabe glanced over his shoulder. His daed working on a coffee table Bishop John had recently ordered for his wife's upcoming birthday.

Maybe I should tell Pap what I'm thinking of doing. Let him know I'm wanting to go out on my own. It wouldn't be right to wait and drop the news on him when the time comes.

Gabe set the sandpaper aside and moved across the room. "Say, Pap, I was wondering if I could talk to you about something."

"Sure, son. What's on your mind?"

Gabe shifted from one foot to the other, his courage beginning to waver. "I've—uh—been thinkin' that I'd like to have my own place of business."

Pap's mouth turned down at the corners. "Are you saying you'd like to open another woodworking business here in our area?"

"Jah."

His daed crossed his arms and stared hard at Gabe. "Would you mind explaining why you'd want to be in competition with me?"

Gabe shook his head. "It wouldn't really be in competition. I'd be makin' other things—stuff like gun stocks, animal cages, birdhouses, and maybe some different kinds of household items, like the trash can holder I've made to give Mom for Christmas."

"Hmm . . . I see."

Gabe felt hope well up in his soul. Maybe Pap understood. "Think you could handle a shop on your own?"

Gabe nodded.

"Guess time will tell." His daed shrugged his shoulders. "In the meanwhile, we've got a job to look at in Branson that'll take a couple of weeks."

"What kind of job?"

"A bed and breakfast needs some new furniture, and they want it to be made by an Amish carpenter."

Gabe leaned against his father's workbench. "What part of the job would you expect me to do?"

"That all depends."

"On what?"

"On what all the customer wants made."

"Who'll we get to drive us to Branson?"

"Don't know yet. Probably Ed Wilkins. He's usually available whenever I need to go somewhere outside the area."

"Jah, okay." Gabe headed back to his own workbench. At least his daed hadn't said he would be stuck doing the menial jobs for the bed and breakfast in Branson. Maybe he would even decide to let Gabe build some of the furniture and not just do the finish work.

"Oh, and Gabe, there's one more thing," Pap called over his shoulder.

"What's that?"

"If it turns out you're still workin' for me after you and Melinda get married, I want you to know that I'll be paying you enough that you can make a decent living."

Gabe sucked in his breath. Should he tell Pap that he and Melinda might not be getting married at all? Would his daed have some good advice if he knew what Gabe was up against right now? Or if Pap knew the whole story, would he be worried that Gabe might decide to leave their Amish community with Melinda?

Gabe grabbed his piece of sandpaper and gave the arm of the chair a couple of good swipes. *I'd best not*

157

be sayin' anything just yet. Better to wait until I know for sure what's what.

By Saturday, Melinda's mother seemed to be feeling better, and she had insisted that she and Melinda pick some produce from the garden. They'd spent most of the morning in the garden harvesting tomatoes and green beans. Now they stood at the kitchen sink washing their bounty of produce.

"You sure you're feelin' up to this, Mama?" Melinda asked with concern. "You were so sick yesterday, and it's probably not a good idea for you to overdo."

Mama waved a hand. "I'm fine, dear one. It was only a twenty-four-hour bug, and I promise to rest awhile once the produce is washed and put away." She smiled. "I want you to know how much I appreciated you canceling your shopping trip and staying home to see to my needs yesterday. That was thoughtful of you, and it just goes to prove what a gut daughter you are."

Melinda's face heated with embarrassment. If her mamm only knew what all she had planned to do in Springfield, she might not be saying such kind things.

"All these tomatoes make me think about that day a few weeks ago when the skunk sprayed you and Gabe," Mama said, taking their conversation in another direction.

"Jah. The two of us smelled to high heavens, and you wouldn't let me come inside until I'd bathed in the galvanized tub Papa Noah had set up in the wood-shed."

Melinda grimaced at the memory of it. After several baths, alternating tomato juice and a mixture of hydrogen peroxide, baking soda, and liquid dish-washing soap, she had scrubbed so hard she was afraid she wouldn't have any skin left.

The day after their spraying, she and Gabe had washed his buggy down with something Dr. Franklin had given her that was stronger than what she'd bathed in. Never again would Melinda knowingly go near another skunk. She was sure Gabe wouldn't, either.

Mama had just placed another batch of tomatoes on a towel to dry when Isaiah entered the room. "Sure glad I didn't have to go to work with Papa Noah today. Pullin' weeds around them trees was harder than workin' in the garden."

"A little hard work never hurt anyone, and I know your daed and Hank Osborn appreciated the help." Mama smiled. "Both of my kinner sacrificed to help others yesterday, and I'm right pleased that we have raised such willing workers. I don't know what I would do without either one of you."

Melinda cringed. *What will Mama say when she finally finds out what I'm thinking of doing? Will she understand why I feel the need to become a vet? Will I feel guilty once I leave home? Can I really give up all that I have here with my family and friends?* She closed her eyes and leaned against the kitchen cup-board. *Oh, Lord, help me to know Your will.*

twenty

Carrying a basket of freshly picked tomatoes, Melinda trudged wearily from the garden to the house. It seemed like there was no end to the ripe tomatoes, and today she and Mama planned to do up several canner-loads. Dr. Franklin had wanted her to work at the clinic this afternoon, but with so many tomatoes yet to be harvested, she felt obligated to lend her mother a hand.

Melinda couldn't believe how much had happened in the last week. She'd finally made it to Springfield last Friday and had taken her GED test. She'd also done some shopping at the discount store. Then last Saturday morning, she had helped her mother bake several loaves of banana bread to take to a couple of widows in their community. In the afternoon, she'd worked at the veterinary clinic. All this week, she had alternated her time between working at the clinic and helping Mama can beans and tomatoes. The truth was, Melinda would have much rather been out in the woods on this Saturday morning sketching some of the wildlife, or inside the chicken coop checking on the baby pheasants that had hatched yesterday morning. She hoped there might still be time for that after they were done for the day.

Melinda had just set her basket of tomatoes on the cupboard and joined her mother at the sink when Isaiah entered the kitchen.

"Mail's here," he announced. "Where do you want it?"

Mama nodded toward the table. "You can put it over there, and then I'd like you to go back outside and pull some weeds in the garden. They're starting to overtake the bean plants."

Isaiah's forehead creased. "How come Melinda didn't pull 'em when she was out there pickin' the produce?"

"I didn't have time for that," Melinda responded before her mother could say anything. "As it is, I'll be busy all afternoon helping Mama put up what I got picked."

"Melinda's right," their mother agreed. "So grab yourself something cold to drink and hurry out to get that weeding done."

Isaiah went to the refrigerator and took out a jug of lemonade. He poured himself a tall glass and headed out the door.

"All right if I take a break to look at the mail?" Melinda asked her mother.

"Sure. I can handle this on my own for a bit."

When Melinda spotted an envelope with the community college's return address, she trembled. It had to be the results of her GED test.

I probably should have had them send it to Dr. Franklin's office, she thought, glancing at her mother, who was still at the sink with her back to Melinda. *But they asked for my home address, and I didn't want to be deceitful by writing down something other than*

161

where I actually live. She cringed. *I've already been deceitful by not telling my folks I took the test or letting them know about my plans for the future. I need to right that wrong, and soon.*

With shaking fingers, Melinda ripped open the envelope. After studying the enclosed scores a few seconds, she sank into the nearest chair with a moan. She'd failed the test.

As she read each section, it became apparent that she had passed the English part of the exam, but the math section had been much harder and she'd missed too many questions. Her only recourse was to study more, then retake the test. Either that, or she would have to give up her dream of going to college and eventually on to veterinary school.

"Anything interesting in the mail today?" Mama asked, breaking into Melinda's swirling thoughts.

"What? Uh—I haven't looked through all of it yet." Melinda slipped the envelope with the GED results inside her apron waistband. If she had passed the test, she would have told Mama her plans, but since she'd failed, she saw no point in mentioning it.

Maybe the Lord is trying to tell me something. Could He want me to give up on the idea of becoming a vet and learn to be content being just an Amish housewife?

She grabbed the rest of the mail and quickly thumbed through it. *Or maybe I'm supposed to be patient and wait awhile longer until I'm more prepared.*

Gabe stared out the back window of the van he and his father rode in. They had hired Ed Wilkins to drive them to Branson this morning, and after meeting with the owners of the bed and breakfast, Papa had signed a contract to make five new tables with matching chairs for their guest kitchen. Gabe wouldn't know until later how much of that job he would be allowed to do, but he had enjoyed his time in the city.

As they traveled along the main street in Branson, he observed several fancy theaters with parking lots full of cars and tour buses. Melinda had told him that this was one of the towns where her mother used to perform, and he wondered if it had been in any of these theaters.

What must it have been like for Faith to live here and be up on stage before an audience, yodeling and telling all kinds of jokes? Does she ever miss it? Would Melinda want to live here if she does become part of the English world again? I'm sure the reason she wants to leave the Amish faith has more to do with her desire to help her animal friends than it does with the allure of the modern world.

"Did you enjoy the lunch we had at the buffet?" Pap asked, breaking into Gabe's thoughts.

Gabe nodded and patted his stomach. "Jah. I had more than my share of peach cobbler and vanilla ice cream at the dessert bar, too."

His daed chuckled. "Same here."

"What have ya got lined up for us to do after we get home this afternoon?" Gabe asked.

"There's a couple of doors that need to be sanded, but since there won't be many hours left to work by the time we get back to the shop, I think you can take the rest of the day off."

"Really? You mean it?"

Pap nodded. "Said so, didn't I?"

Gabe smiled. He figured if he headed straight for the woods after they got home, he'd have plenty of time to do some target practicing before Mom had supper ready.

Melinda tromped through the tall grass, making her way to the woods behind their house. She was glad to finally have some time to be off by herself. All day, as she and Mama had canned tomatoes, she'd grieved over failing her test. Maybe some time in the woods with the wildlife she liked so much would help her gain some perspective and relieve the disappointment.

As Melinda passed the deer feeder Gabe had made, she wondered if she could survive in the English world without him. She hadn't seen Gabe for a couple of weeks, but he had left a note in the birdhouse yesterday saying he and his *daed* would be going to Branson to look at a job today. Melinda wished she could have gone along. She hadn't been back to Branson since she was a little girl. She'd asked about going a couple of times during her growing up years, but Mama always said that Branson was part of her past and that she had no desire to go there again.

As Melinda stepped into the woods, her mind whirled with confusion. *English or Amish? Forget about taking another GED test or try again? Marry Gabe or become a vet?*

She shook her head, trying to clear away the troubling thoughts. Three deer—a buck and two does—showed up on the scene, and she quickly took a seat on a tree stump.

Melinda pulled her drawing tablet and pencil out of the canvas bag she'd brought along, and for the next hour she watched in fascination as she sketched the beautiful creatures.

Pop! Pop! Pop! She tipped her head. It sounded like a gun. But that was impossible. It wasn't deer hunting season yet. Besides, Papa Noah had posted No Hunting signs on their property. Someone would have to be pretty dumb to be hunting on their land.

Pop! Pop! The sound came again, a little closer this time. The deer bolted into the bushes, and Melinda groaned. *Just one more thing to ruin my day.*

She tossed her artwork into the canvas satchel, slung it over her shoulder, and headed toward the gunfire, keeping low and, hopefully, out of danger. Whoever was doing the shooting was in for a good tongue-lashing.

A few minutes later, she halted. Gabe stood next to her little brother, and Isaiah held a gun in his hands!

She marched over to them, jerked the gun away from Isaiah, and thrust it at Gabe. "What are you doing here?"

"I've been showing Isaiah how to shoot."

Melinda's heart pounded, and her mouth felt so dry she could barely speak. "What would make you do such a thing?"

"Isaiah saw the gun stock I made for Aaron when he was over at the Zooks' playing with Aaron's younger brothers," Gabe explained. "When he and your daed dropped by our shop the other day, Isaiah asked if I'd be willing to teach him how to shoot."

"Did my stepdaed agree to that?" Melinda's question was directed at Gabe, but it was Isaiah who responded.

"When I spoke to Gabe about shootin' a gun, Papa was busy talkin' to Gabe's daed. I didn't think he'd mind, seein' as how I'm twelve years old now." Isaiah looked at Melinda as though daring her to say otherwise. "I can go huntin' with a youth permit as long as I'm with an adult who's licensed to hunt."

Melinda's attention snapped back to Gabe. "But you said you were giving up hunting."

He frowned. "I never said that."

"You told me you were sorry about our disagreement and that—"

"I was sorry. Sorry we had words, but not sorry for shootin' my gun." His jaw clenched, and the late afternoon shadows shifted on his cheek. "I don't see anything wrong with hunting deer when it's for food, not just a trophy."

Melinda realized Gabe was right. He hadn't actually said he wouldn't hunt anymore. She had just assumed that's what he meant when he apologized. And after he gave her the deer feeder he'd made, she thought he felt the same way about the forest animals as she did. She also knew that many men hunted deer for food, not just the sport of it. Even though she couldn't save every deer in the woods, the ones in these woods were hers, and she didn't want any of them hurt. She also didn't like the idea of Gabe teaching her little brother how to hunt.

"It's obvious to me," she said in a shaky voice, "that you don't care nearly as much about animals as I do, which is probably why you won't—"

Gabe held up his hand and nodded toward Isaiah.

Melinda knew it wasn't a good idea to discuss their problems in front of her little brother. In her irritation with Gabe, she'd almost forgotten Isaiah was still here.

"You'd better head for home," she told her brother.

He jutted out his chin. "You ain't my boss."

Melinda opened her mouth to respond, but Gabe cut her off. "Isaiah, I think it would be best if you did go home. Your folks might be missing you by now."

Melinda was tempted to tell Gabe he should have thought about that before he dragged her little brother into the woods and placed a gun in his hands, but she decided to keep quiet. Enough had already been said in front of Isaiah, and she didn't want him going home and spouting off about everything he'd heard her and Gabe say.

"Okay, I'll go," Isaiah said, "but only because you

asked me nice, Gabe." He cast a quick glance at Melinda and wrinkled his nose.

Melinda folded her arms and said nothing.

"Maybe we can target practice some other time," Isaiah said, smiling at Gabe.

"We'll have to wait and see how it goes," Gabe replied.

"Jah, okay." Isaiah turned toward home.

Melinda waited until he was out of sight before she spoke again. Then drawing in a deep breath to steady her nerves, she looked right at Gabe. "You don't have to worry about me leaving the Amish faith. At least not any time soon."

He blinked a couple of times as though he didn't quite believe her.

"I failed my GED test."

"You did?"

She nodded.

"So you've given up on the idea of becoming a vet?"

"Well, I—"

"It's for the best, Melinda. You'll see that once we're married."

Melinda drew back like a turtle being poked with a sharp stick. "You don't even care that I failed, do you?"

"Of course I do, but—"

"You know what I think, Gabe?"

He shook his head.

"Even if I were to stay Amish and we did get married, we would probably always be arguing."

"I don't think so, Melinda."

"Jah, we would. We'd argue about all my pets that you think are silly. We'd argue about whether it's all right for you to hunt or not. We'd argue about—" Melinda's throat felt too clogged to say anything more. All she wanted to do was run for the safety of home, and that's exactly what she did.

twenty-one

Gabe watched Melinda's retreating form. He'd made such a mess of things. It seemed as though that's all he did anymore—clutter everything between them and make her upset. "I never should have brought Isaiah into the woods to target practice," Gabe mumbled. "Especially not without gettin' Noah's permission." He gathered up his gun and ammunition. "This whole thing between me and Melinda stinks about as bad as when the two of us got sprayed by a skunk!"

Gabe knew the first thing he needed to do was apologize to Melinda's stepfather. Then he had to come up with some way to patch things up with Melinda. There had to be something he could do to make her realize how much he loved her. Either that, or they would have to go their separate ways, which seemed to be what she wanted to do.

Gabe swallowed around the lump in his throat and started walking toward the Hertzlers' place. He had been in love with Melinda too long to let their relationship go, no matter how much they disagreed on things.

• • •

Melinda paced the length of the front porch, waiting for Papa Noah to show up. He had worked at the Christmas tree farm today because Hank Osborn was shorthanded. Usually Papa Noah had Saturdays off, but he always made himself available whenever his boss had a need.

Melinda thought about the tree farm and how much she'd enjoyed visiting there when she was a girl. It had been exciting to see the many rows of various sizes of pine trees that would eventually become some English person's Christmas tree. But she hadn't visited Osborn's Tree Farm in several years.

I don't need to look at Christmas trees anymore. Not when I've got a whole forest full of beautiful trees I can gaze at whenever I want.

She glanced at the darkening sky, knowing she needed to go inside and see if her mother needed any help, but just then her stepfather's buggy rolled into the yard.

Melinda bounded off the porch and sprinted out to the buggy just in time to see Gabe walking across the open field between their house and the woods. She hurried to Papa Noah's side as soon as he stepped down from the buggy. "I need to tell you something," she panted.

"What is it? You look upset."

"I discovered Isaiah and Gabe in the woods together awhile ago, and you'll never guess what they were doing."

"What was it?"

"Gabe was teaching Isaiah to shoot a gun."

Papa Noah's eyebrows furrowed. "He was?"

She nodded.

Before Papa Noah could say anything more, Gabe stepped between them, all red-faced and sweaty. "I—I need to speak with you, Noah."

"What'd you want to say?"

"When Isaiah asked me to teach him to shoot, I figured he'd gotten your permission and that you had a youth permit for him." Gabe gave Melinda a sidelong glance, but she looked away.

"Isaiah has never said a word to me about wanting to hunt or even asked about shooting a gun," Papa Noah said.

"I'm sorry. I should have asked you first, and please know that it will never happen again." Gabe's expression was somber, but Melinda couldn't help but wonder if he really was sorry. Maybe he was simply trying to keep himself out of trouble with her stepfather.

"I accept your apology, Gabe," Papa Noah said, "and I thank you for having the courage to come talk to me about this matter." He glanced over at Melinda. "I need to put my horse away. Would you please tell your mamm I'll be in for supper soon?"

She nodded. "I'll give her the message."

Papa Noah headed for the barn, and Melinda turned toward the house, but she had only taken a few steps when Gabe touched her shoulder. "Listen, about our disagreement—"

She halted and turned around.

"I'm sorry about your GED. I understand how much it meant to you."

Melinda shook her head. "I don't think you do understand, Gabe. If you did, you might be more willing to do some things just for me."

"Like what?"

She pointed to the gun in his hands.

"I wasn't plannin' to hunt on your property."

"I don't care where you had planned to hunt. You shouldn't be teaching Isaiah to hunt. He's too young."

"Not if he has a youth permit and hunts with your daed."

"Papa Noah doesn't hunt, and to my knowledge he never has."

Gabe stared at the ground, kicking small rocks with the toe of his boot. "The truth is, you really don't want me to hunt. Isn't that right?"

"I know we need some animals for meat," she said, avoiding his question.

He nodded. "That's true. There's even a list of those animals in the Bible."

"But the deer are very special to me."

"I know. The deer and every other critter you want to help." He stared at her with such intensity, she thought he might break down and cry. "The simple fact is, you care so much about animals that you'd be willing to give up your faith, family, and friends in order to care for them the way Doc Franklin does."

"Gabe, I—"

"And you want me to give up all those things so we can be together."

Tears welled up in Melinda's eyes. Gabe was right. She did want that. In fact, she thought that if he was willing to leave the Amish faith, it would prove how much he loved her.

"Even if we both left our home here in Webster County, things would never feel right between us," he said with a catch in his voice.

"What do you mean?"

"I'd be leaving family and friends, and so would you."

"I know that, and the thought of it pains me, Gabe. But we would have each other, and eventually we'd have a family of our own."

"I'd have to give up my dream of owning my own woodworking business, too."

She shook her head. "You could do carpentry work in the English world."

He took a step toward her. "I love you, Melinda, and I always will, but it's time I face the fact that your wants and my wants don't mesh. I'm sorry to say this, but I finally realize that it's over between us." Gabe swung around and bolted from the yard.

With tears coursing down her cheeks, Melinda moved slowly toward the house. Gabe was right. They both wanted different things. As much as it pained her to admit the truth, they had no future together.

It was difficult for Melinda to attend church at the Hiltys' place the next day, but unless she was sick, there was no way she could get out of going. After what had happened yesterday, she didn't want to face Gabe.

Melinda had just stepped down from the buggy when Susie rushed up to her. "Is it true, Melinda? Have you and Gabe really broken up for good?"

"I can't believe the news is out already," Melinda muttered. "Who told you?"

"Gabe must have told his mother, and then she told my mamm when they got here a few minutes ago." Susie eyed Melinda critically. "Please tell me it's not true."

Melinda quickly explained the way she had discovered Gabe teaching Isaiah how to shoot and how Gabe had broken things off.

Susie's expression was solemn. "I can't believe you'd be so *narrisch*. Don't you realize how much Gabe loves you?"

"I'm not being foolish." Melinda shrugged. "And I guess Gabe doesn't love me as much as I had thought."

Susie touched Melinda's arm. "Have you prayed about this? Maybe there's something you can say or do to make Gabe change his mind."

Melinda shook her head as tears clouded her vision. "I would have to give up caring for animals if we did get back together."

Susie's eyebrows lifted. "Why would you have to do that? You're caring for animals now, aren't you?"

Melinda didn't know how to respond. It was true—

she was caring for some animals but in such a small way. It was nothing like how she could help them if she became a vet.

"We'd better get inside," she said, moving toward the house. "There's no point in discussing this more, and church will be starting soon."

"You look like you've been suckin' on a bunch of sour grapes," Aaron said to Gabe as they climbed down from their buggies at the same time.

Gabe moved to the front of his buggy and started to unhitch the horse. "Yesterday Melinda and I broke up."

Aaron skirted around his own rig. "You're kidding, right?'

"No, it's the truth."

"But, I thought you two were crazy in love."

"I used to think that, too."

"What happened, then?"

"Melinda caught me in the woods out behind their place teachin' her little brother how to shoot a gun."

Aaron reached under his hat and scratched the side of his head. "That's all there is? She broke up with you because of that?"

"Actually, it was me who broke up with her, but I think she agrees that things could never work out between us." Gabe grabbed his horse's bridle and led him toward the corral where other horses milled about.

Aaron followed, leaving his own horse still hitched

to the buggy. "That's the dumbest thing I've ever heard. If you love the woman, why don't you fight for her?"

"Melinda's love for animals has come between us," he said. "She doesn't want me to hunt." Gabe was tempted to tell his friend the rest of the story, but he figured Aaron might blab to someone else about Melinda wanting to become a vet, so he decided to keep that to himself.

"That's ridiculous! She can't save every deer in the woods. Melinda's got *verhuddled* thinking."

"It might be confused thinking to you and me, but it isn't to her."

Aaron leaned against the corral while Gabe put his horse inside. "So what are you gonna do about this?"

Gabe turned his hands palm up. "What can I do?"

You can give up hunting, a little voice whispered inside his head. *You can leave the Amish faith to help Melinda fulfill her dream.*

"I know what I would do," Aaron said.

"What's that?"

"I'd tell Melinda she's verhuddled and that she needs to come to her senses."

Gabe shook his head. "That would only make things worse. The only thing I can do at this point is to pray about our situation."

"You never know, Melinda might change her mind about you hunting. Women are prone to that, ya know," Aaron said with a serious expression.

Gabe gave his horse a gentle pat and left the corral.

"You'd best get your horse in here. Church will be starting soon."

"You're right." Aaron followed Gabe back to his horse and buggy. "This whole ordeal you're goin' through with Melinda is exactly why I'm never gettin' married!"

Gabe nodded. Maybe Aaron had the right idea about marriage. Maybe it would have been better if he'd never fallen in love with Melinda.

twenty-two

Melinda didn't know why she had let Susie talk her into attending the singing tonight, but here she sat, alone on a bale of straw in Abe Martin's barn. It was hard to watch other couples as they paired off and engaged in singing lively songs and sharing friendly banter. Everyone but her seemed to be having a good time. How could she enjoy herself when she wasn't with Gabe and wouldn't be riding home in his buggy at the close of the evening?

It might have been easier if Gabe hadn't been at the singing, but there he was in front of the punch bowl talking to Katie Byler. Had he found a replacement for her so soon? The thought of Gabe courting someone else made Melinda's stomach feel queasy, and unbidden tears sprang to her eyes. She sniffed and swiped them away just as Susie plunked down beside her.

"Guess what?"

Susie seemed excited about something, but in

Melinda's glum mood, it was all she could do to respond with a shrug.

"Jonas Byler asked if he could give me a ride home in his buggy tonight."

"Katie's brother?"

"Jah. Jonas is five years older than me, and until now he's never given me so much as a second glance."

"Where's Jonas been these last few years?" Melinda asked. "I heard he left home some time ago."

"He's been living in northern Montana with a group of Amish there, but he recently moved back to Webster County." Susie smiled. "Maybe Jonas sees me in a different light now and realizes I'm not a little girl anymore."

"Either that or he got tired of the bitter Montana winters and decided to return to his roots."

"Our winters can get cold, too," Susie said in a defensive tone.

"That's true."

"It might be that Jonas just missed bein' around his family and friends. I hear tell many Amish who move to remote settlements like those in Montana don't stay very long." Susie popped a couple of her knuckles, the way Melinda's mother often did. "Fact is, Jonas told me there hasn't been a single Amish person born and raised in the Rexford, Montana, area who decided to stay for good. He says people come and go, but some have stayed longer than others."

Melinda broke off a piece of straw and clenched it between her teeth.

"I've never traveled much and would sure like the chance to see some of the states out west," Susie went on to say. "Jonas says the Amish who live in northern Montana have log homes, only they're much nicer than those the pioneers used to live in."

Melinda listened halfheartedly as her aunt droned on about Montana and how she couldn't wait to spend more time with Jonas. It was hard for Melinda to concentrate on anything other than Gabe and Katie, who stood off by themselves in one corner of the barn.

I wonder if he's doing that to make me jealous. He probably thinks if I believe he's interested in someone else, I'll say it's okay for him to hunt and I'll stay Amish and won't even try to retake my GED or become a vet. Melinda clenched her fingers into tight balls and held them firmly in her lap. "Maybe I ought to move to Montana," she muttered.

Susie nudged her arm. "What was that?"

"Oh, nothing." Melinda stood, smoothing the wrinkles in her dark blue dress. "I think I'll take a walk outside and get some fresh air."

"Want some company?"

"If Jonas plans to take you home tonight, you'd better stay put. I wouldn't want you to miss out on your first date with him because of me."

"I'm sure he won't leave without me. Besides, the singing's not over yet."

"Just the same, I'd rather be alone if you don't mind."

Susie shrugged. "Suit yourself."

Melinda noticed Jonas heading their way with two

glasses of punch, so she hurried off. At least Susie was having a good time this evening, and she deserved to be happy.

Outside, Melinda wandered around the yard, staring up at the sky and studying the thousands of brilliant stars. *I probably shouldn't have come here tonight.* Tears spilled onto her cheeks. *If only Gabe and I could work things out.*

The scripture verse Philippians 2:3 popped into her mind: *"Let nothing be done through strife or vainglory; but in lowliness of mind let each esteem other better than themselves."*

More tears came, and Melinda reached up to wipe them away. She knew she hadn't put Gabe's needs ahead of hers. But shouldn't he care about her feelings, too? If Gabe really loved her, then why couldn't he see how much she wanted to help hurting animals, and why wouldn't he reconsider leaving the Amish faith with her so she could do it?

"How come you're out here by yourself?"

Melinda whirled around at the sound of a deep voice. In the light of the full moon, she realized it was Gabe's friend, Aaron. "I—I'm just getting some fresh air."

He grunted. "Jah, fresh and chilly. Fall's right around the corner, and soon winter will be here."

"I assume that winter's not your favorite time of the year?"

He shrugged. "I can take it or leave it. But to tell ya the truth, I prefer warmer days when I can go fishin'."

Melinda rubbed her hands briskly over her arms. Aaron was right, it was kind of nippy out tonight.

"I was sorry to hear about you and Gabe breakin' up," Aaron said. "Seems a shame you two can't find some way to work out your differences."

A lump formed in Melinda's throat, and she swallowed to push it down. "He doesn't understand how I feel about things."

"Seems to me that you don't understand him, either."

Melinda cringed. Had Gabe told Aaron all the details of their breakup? He must have, or Aaron wouldn't have said such a thing. Now everyone would soon know, and she wasn't sure she was ready to deal with that. Especially since she still hadn't told her parents any of the details.

"Uh, Aaron, please don't say anything to anyone about me wanting to leave the faith, okay?"

"Huh?"

"I haven't told my folks I'm thinking about becoming a vet, so—"

"Whoa!" Aaron held up his hand. "You're thinking of what?"

"I—thought you knew. From what you'd said earlier, I figured Gabe must have told you everything."

Aaron let out a low whistle. "Now I know why he seemed so upset."

"You mean he didn't tell you what I'm thinking of doing?"

He shook his head. "Just said you'd broken up because he wants to hunt and you're opposed to the idea."

Melinda felt like someone had punched her in the stomach. Aaron hadn't known the truth until she'd opened her mouth and blabbed the whole thing. Now he might tell others, and then things could get really sticky.

She glanced to the left and caught sight of two people walking toward one of the open buggies. Her heart plummeted when she realized it was Gabe and Katie. When Gabe helped Katie into the passenger's seat, then climbed up beside her, Melinda trembled. *It hurts to know he's gotten over me so quickly.*

She turned away, unable to watch the couple drive off together.

"Sorry you had to see that," Aaron said.

"I'd better get used to it, because from the way things look, Gabe will probably marry someone else and I'll be—" Her voice caught on a sob. "Oh, please, Aaron, don't say anything to anyone about the things I have shared with you tonight."

He shook his head. "That ain't for me to be sayin', Melinda."

"Danki. I appreciate that." She sighed. "Sure wish the singing was over and I could go home. Papa Noah won't come to pick me up until ten o'clock. I've got a headache and don't think I can make it through the rest of the evening."

"I'd be glad to give you a lift home right now," Aaron offered. "It would save your daed a trip and keep you from havin' to stick around here."

Melinda sniffed. "I'd hate for you to miss all the fun on account of me."

"Nah. I wasn't havin' much fun anyway."

"Are you sure? I mean, isn't there someone else you'd rather escort home?"

Aaron shook his head, then chuckled embarrassedly. "If I do ever find a woman, she'll have to be spunky like my mamm. I'd want someone who likes to fish and isn't afraid to get her hands dirty."

"Most Amish women I know do lots in their gardens. Doesn't that count as dirty work?"

"I reckon so, but that's not what I meant." Aaron led Melinda toward his buggy.

"What did you mean?"

He tipped his head to one side. "Any woman I'd ever consider marryin' would have to be willin' to do some outdoor stuff."

"Oh, you mean she should be a tomboy?"

Aaron shrugged. "Guess that's one way to put it, but that ain't likely to happen, 'cause there's no women around here that I'd be interested in." He helped her into his buggy and took his place in the driver's seat.

"Well, Aaron Zook," Melinda said with a groan, "I hope you have better luck at finding love than I've had."

Melinda lay in bed that night thinking and praying. Did Aaron have the right attitude about staying single? If she left home to become a veterinarian, she would probably stay single unless she met and married some English fellow. That thought did nothing to make her feel better. She'd been miserable since she and Gabe had broken up, but she saw no way they could get back together unless one of them made a huge concession.

Gabe would probably be better off with Katie. She's so cute. Cute, and she wants to remain Amish.

twenty-three

"I came by to check on some kitchen cabinets I ordered to give Faith for Christmas," Noah Hertzler said when he stepped into Swartz's Woodworking Shop.

Gabe leaned against his workbench and crossed his arms. "My daed's off delivering some furniture right now, but I know your cabinets have been made and are waiting to be sanded and stained. I'm sure they'll be ready for Christmas." He thought about all the orders they had for holiday gifts and about how Pap had allowed him to make some chairs and a table for the bed and breakfast in Branson. They'd turned out well, and Pap had said he was really pleased with Gabe's work.

"Glad to hear the cabinets will be ready soon, because the ones in our kitchen were bought used when we built the house next to my folks' place," Noah said, jolting Gabe out of his musings. "They need to be replaced, and my wife's been wantin' new ones for quite some time." Noah shifted from one foot to the other, as though he might have something more to say. "I—uh—wanted to tell you that I'm real sorry

184

to hear about you and Melinda breakin' up. I like you, Gabe, and was lookin' forward to hopefully havin' you as my son-in-law." He handed Gabe a plate of chocolate-chip cookies wrapped with cellophane. "I made these last night and thought you might like some."

"Danki. That was nice of you." Gabe placed the cookies on one end of his workbench. The truth was, he thought highly of Melinda's daed and figured he'd probably make a good father-in-law.

Noah placed his hands on the front of the work-bench and leaned toward Gabe. "Melinda's been actin' like a kitten with a sore paw ever since you two split up. Spends most of her time with those critters of hers, and Faith is fit to be tied because she has to prod the gal to get any work done."

Gabe pondered Noah's words before responding. "If she's so concerned about going our separate ways, then why'd she ride home from the last singing with my best friend?"

"You mean Aaron Zook?"

"Jah."

"I didn't know that. Thought one of the girls who had no date had given Melinda a ride that night. I was supposed to pick her up, but she arrived home way before ten." Noah looked intently at Gabe. "I'm thinkin' this is something you and Melinda need to discuss. Don't believe she'd like the idea of me buttin' in on something that's really none of my busi-ness."

185

"There's a lot more going on than just her riding home with Aaron."

Noah nodded. "If you're talkin' about her not wanting you to hunt, she explained her reasons to me, and I told her she was wrong."

Gabe toyed with a piece of sandpaper, pushing it back and forth across the work space in front of him even though there was nothing there to sand. "That's not the whole issue here, but it's not for me to be saying. Melinda will tell you everything when she's ready, I'm sure." He drew in a deep breath and released it with a huff. "I'm afraid it's too late for anything to be resolved between Melinda and me."

Noah shook his head. "It's never too late. Not as long as you're both still free to marry." He turned toward the door but called over his shoulder, "My daughter's worth fighting for."

The door clicked shut, and Gabe's gaze came to rest on the cookies Noah had left him. It was then that he noticed a verse of Scripture had been attached to the edge of the cellophane. He reached for it and read the words out loud. " 'But the wisdom that is from above is first pure, then peaceable, gentle, and easy to be intreated, full of mercy and good fruits, without partiality, and without hypocrisy. And the fruit of righteousness is sown in peace of them that make peace.' "

What was Noah trying to tell him? Did he think Gabe should try and make peace with Melinda? He wasn't sure there was any way they could get back to where they had been before she'd told him she wanted to become a vet, but he would continue to pray about the matter.

Early this morning, Melinda's mother had hired a driver and taken Grandpa to Springfield for a doctor appointment, asking Melinda to do some cleaning before she left for work at noon. True to her promise, Melinda was now mopping the kitchen floor.

She glanced at the calendar on the opposite wall. It had been two weeks since she and Gabe had gone their separate ways, and the pain in her heart was still raw.

Dear Lord, bless Gabe and bring him happiness even if it ends up to be Katie Byler who makes him happy. And give me wisdom and direction for my life. Help me know whether I should take another GED test or not.

Loud barking in the backyard interrupted Melinda's prayer. She set the mop aside and peeked out the window, wondering what Isaiah's dog was up to now. But it wasn't her brother's hound she saw in the yard. It was Gabe's German shepherd, Shep, running around in circles and barking like crazy.

Melinda opened the back door and stepped onto the porch. "What's the matter with you, Shep? You act like you've been stung by a swarm of bees."

As soon as Melinda spoke, the dog quit running and crawled toward the house.

"What's wrong, boy?" She stepped off the porch. "Are you hurt?"

Shep's only response was a pathetic whimper.

As Melinda drew closer, she realized Shep had several porcupine quills stuck in his nose. "Looks like you had a run in with an angry critter, didn't you? We need to get those out right away."

The dog looked up at Melinda with sorrowful brown eyes. "Come on, fella. Let's go to the barn and get that taken care of." She led the way, and obediently the dog followed.

A short time later, after removing the quills with a pair of pliers, Melinda was putting antiseptic on Shep's nose when an unexpected visitor showed up. It was Gabe, and as he stepped into the barn, the stubble of straw crackled under his weight. "I've been lookin' everywhere for you, Shep." He glanced at Melinda. "The critter took off last night. I figured he'd come over here to play with Isaiah's dog, but he didn't return, and this morning I got worried." Gabe frowned. "What's wrong with him? Why are you doctorin' my dog?"

Melinda set the bottle of peroxide back on the shelf before she answered. "I found him in the backyard barking and running around in circles, and I discovered that he had a bunch of porcupine quills stuck in his nose."

Gabe patted his knee, and the dog went immediately to his side. "You silly critter. I thought you had more sense than to tangle with a porcupine."

Shep licked Gabe's hand and whined.

"Sure appreciate you lookin' out for him," Gabe said. "Guess Shep was smart enough to know who to come to when he needed help."

Melinda smiled. "Animals have a sixth sense about things."

Gabe took hold of Shep's collar and led him toward the barn door. "Guess I'd better get back home. Pap's at the shop by himself, and we've got a lot of work to do."

"It's kind of chilly this morning. Would you like a cup of hot chocolate before you go?" Melinda asked.

He licked his lips. "Hot chocolate sounds nice. If you've got a couple of marshmallows to go with it, that is." He grinned at Melinda, and her heart skipped a beat.

"I think there's some marshmallows in the kitchen cupboard. Why don't you put Shep in the dog run with Jericho, and I'll meet you on the back porch."

"Sounds gut to me."

For the next little while, Gabe and Melinda sat in chairs on the porch sipping hot chocolate and making small talk. Gabe wanted to discuss their relationship, but he couldn't seem to work up the nerve.

"How's Katie Byler?" Melinda blurted suddenly.

Gabe nearly choked on the warm liquid in his mouth. "Huh?"

"I said, how's Katie Byler?"

He shrugged and reached up to wipe away the chocolate that had dribbled onto his chin. "I guess she's okay. Why do you ask?"

Melinda's cheeks were bright pink, and he didn't

think it had anything to do with the weather. "I saw the two of you together at the last singing, and I also know you took her home."

"I didn't hang around Katie all night at the singing," he said defensively. "I just talked to her a few minutes after we both had some punch."

"But I saw her get into your buggy, and you were obviously driving her home."

He nodded. "That's true. Katie told me her brother Jonas was plannin' to ask your aunt Susie if she'd be willing to ride in his buggy after the singing was over."

"What's that got to do with you taking Katie home?"

"I'm gettin' to that." Gabe set his empty cup on the porch floor. "Katie mentioned that she'd come down with a headache and wanted to go home. Since her brother wouldn't be driving Susie home until the singing was over, Katie had no transportation."

"So you volunteered to drive her?"

"Jah."

Melinda stared at her empty cup. "Guess I must have gotten the wrong impression."

"There's nothing going on with me and Katie. We're just friends, and I was only doing a good deed that night." Gabe squinted. "While we're on the subject of rides home from the singing . . . I heard you rode with Aaron."

She nodded. "It's true."

"Are you two seeing each other now?"

She shook her head so hard the ties on her kapp came loose. "Of course not. Aaron only gave me a ride

190

because I, too, had a headache and wanted to go. Papa Noah was supposed to pick me up, but I didn't want to wait around until the singing was over."

Gabe smiled as a feeling of relief washed over him. "I'm glad to hear that."

"What? That I had a headache?"

"No, that you and Aaron aren't seeing each other."

"I'm not interested in Aaron," she said in a near whisper.

Gabe leaned a bit closer and was tempted to kiss her, but a ruckus in the dog run ruined the mood.

"I hope they're not fighting over the bone I gave Jericho last night." Melinda jumped up and bounded off the porch.

Gabe followed. "I'd best get my dog and head for home."

A few minutes later, Gabe had Shep out of the pen and loaded into the back of his buggy. As he pulled out of the driveway, he waved, and Melinda lifted her hand in response. Even though things weren't back to where they should be, at least she was speaking to him again.

"How'd things go with Grandpa's appointment today?" Melinda asked her mother that evening as they prepared supper.

"The results of his blood tests were good," Mama replied, "and the doctor was pleased with how well Grandpa is doing."

Melinda smiled. "Jah. He certainly has made a turn-around, especially where his memory is concerned."

Mama handed her a sack of flour. "Would you mind making some biscuits while I fry up the chicken?"

"Sure, I can do that."

Melinda and her mother worked in silence for a time. Then Mama turned the gas burner under the pan of chicken down and nodded toward the table. "Want to sit awhile and have a cup of tea while the meat cooks and the biscuit dough rises?"

"That sounds gut."

"How'd your day go?" Mama asked as she poured them both a cup of lemon-mint tea.

"It was busy. Started out with me doing the cleaning you'd wanted done, and then Gabe's dog showed up with a bunch of porcupine quills stuck in his nose."

"Ouch! I'll bet that hurt."

Melinda nodded. "I'm sure it did. I removed them with a pair of pliers and put some antiseptic on his nose, and by the time Gabe took Shep home, he was actin' his old spunky self."

Mama's eyebrows lifted. "Did Gabe bring the dog over for you to doctor then?"

"No. Shep came on his own, and Gabe showed up later, lookin' for him."

Her mother took a sip of tea and blotted her lips on a napkin. "How'd that go? Did the two of you get anything resolved?"

Melinda shrugged. "Not really, but we didn't argue, either."

"That's a gut thing. Maybe if you give yourselves a

bit more time, you'll be able to settle your differences."

Melinda was about to comment when Snow came whizzing into the room with something white between her teeth."

"What's that crazy cat got now?" Mama leaned over and squinted as Snow sailed under the table. "Looks like a hunk of balled up paper."

Melinda chuckled. "Well, at least it's not a mouse."

"Here, kitty. Let me have a look-see at what's in your mouth," her mother said, reaching for the cat.

Melinda didn't know who was more surprised, her or Mama, when Snow dropped the balled up piece of paper.

"Well, what do you know—she listened to me for once," Mama said with laugh. She bent down and picked up the paper, pulling it apart with her fingers and laying it flat on the table. "What's this?"

Melinda froze as her gaze came to rest on the item in question. It was the results of her failed GED test.

Mama's forehead wrinkled as she studied the piece of paper, then she looked pointedly at Melinda.

"I—I can explain," Melinda said in a near whisper.

"I hope so."

Melinda moistened her lips with the tip of her tongue. "Uh—as you know, Dr. Franklin thinks I have a special way with animals."

Mama nodded.

"And he believes I would make a good vet or even a certified veterinarian's assistant."

No response.

"And—well, he suggested I take the GED test, which I would need in order to sign up for some college classes."

"You want to go to college and become a vet?" Her mother's voice was calm and even, but Melinda could see by the pinched expression on her face that Mama was having a hard time keeping her emotions under control.

"As you can see by the scores on that paper, I failed the test."

"Does that mean you've given up on the idea then?"

Melinda toyed with the handle on her teacup. "I—I'm not sure, Mama. I've thought about retaking the test."

Her mother released a deep sigh. "And you've been planning all of this behind your daed's and my back, sneaking off to take the test without ever saying a word about any of your plans."

Melinda's eyes filled with tears as a wave of shame and regret washed over her. "I was planning to tell you."

"When?"

"After I passed the GED test."

Mama grabbed two fingers on her left hand and gave them a good pop. "Have you thought about what it would mean if you went off to college and got a degree? Have you thought about how it would affect everyone in this family?"

"Of course I have, and it wouldn't be easy to leave home." There was a tremor in Melinda's voice, and it was all she could do to look her mamm in the face.

"After all the things I've told you about my life as an entertainer, I wouldn't think you would even consider becoming part of the English world." Her mother sniffed, and her quivering chin let Melinda know that she was close to tears. "Not when all your family and friends are Amish, living here in Webster County."

Melinda sat there staring at her untouched cup of tea. "I—I don't want to leave home, Mama, but becoming a vet would allow me to care for so many hurting or sick animals. And if I have a special touch with animals, as Dr. Franklin says, wouldn't it be wasted if I didn't learn how to care for them in the best possible way?"

"Then I guess what it comes down to is, you're going to have to choose which is more important to you—the animals that you think need your help or your family and friends who love you so much."

Melinda blinked against the tears making her vision seem hazy, but she made no comment.

Mama leaned across the table and looked at her long and hard. "I'm not saying these things to make you feel guilty, daughter. I just don't want you to make the same mistake as I did when I left home." She slid her chair back and stood. "Please know that as much as I would hate to see you go, I won't try to stop you. It's your life, and you will have to decide."

"Danki, I appreciate that."

Mama patted Melinda on the shoulder. "Now I need to see about that chicken."

For several seconds, Melinda sat feeling as if she were in a stupor. *I should have told Mama sooner— maybe even had Dr. Franklin talk to her and Papa Noah.*

"I—uh—need to check on my animals in the barn," she said, pushing away from the table.

When her mother made no reply, Melinda rushed out the back door and headed straight for the barn. At least there she might find some solace.

twenty-four

It was the first day of deer hunting season, and as the Hertzlers sat at the breakfast table, Noah instructed Melinda and Isaiah to stay out of the woods.

"But, Papa Noah, there's NO HUNTING signs posted all over our property," Melinda reminded him.

"That's true," he said, "but there's always someone who either doesn't see the signs or refuses to take them seriously and hunts wherever he pleases."

"Yep, that's right," Grandpa put in. "Why I remember when I was a boy, someone shot a deer right out in our front yard."

Melinda clenched her teeth. She hoped the deer on their property would be okay and stay where it was safe.

All morning as Melinda did her chores, she worried about the deer. By the time she had finished cleaning the kitchen, she was a ball of nerves.

Maybe a walk in the woods would make me feel

196

better, she told herself as she dried and placed the last glass in the cupboard.

"Stay out of the woods." Papa Noah's earlier warning echoed in her ears.

I'll only be there a short time. Just long enough to check on the deer.

She glanced around the room. No sign of Mama or Grandpa, and she knew Isaiah wasn't here, because right after breakfast he'd said he was going fishing over at Rabers' pond. Papa Noah had left for work as soon as they were finished eating, and she figured her mother had gone next door to help Grandpa with something in his kitchen.

As Melinda hung up her choring apron, she thought about her discussion with her mamm just a few days ago, and how since that time there had been no mention of her failed GED test or any possible plans of Melinda becoming a vet. She wasn't sure if Mama had said anything to Papa Noah about it, because so far he hadn't said a word.

"I'd better leave Mama a note," she murmured, "so she doesn't worry if she returns to the house and finds me gone." She hurried over to the table and scrawled a message on the tablet there, saying simply that she was going for a short walk before it was time to leave for the clinic. Then she rushed out the back door.

Fifteen minutes later, Melinda stepped into the thicket of trees, wishing she had remembered to bring along her drawing tablet.

It's probably for the best. If I took the time to draw,

I would get carried away and be here much longer than I should.

The sound of gunfire in the distance caused Melinda to shudder. Some poor animal had probably met its fate. Well, at least it hadn't happened on their property.

She walked deeper into the woods, savoring the distinct aroma of fall with its crisp, clean air and fresh-fallen leaves strewn on the ground like a carpet of gold.

The rustle of leaves halted Melinda's footsteps. She tipped her head and listened. There it was again.

She scanned the area but saw nothing out of the ordinary. Suddenly a fawn stepped out of the bushes and stood there staring at Melinda as though it needed her help.

Melinda took a step forward, then another and another, until she was right beside the little deer. That's when she saw it—a doe lying dead among a clump of bushes. "Oh no!" Her breath caught in her throat.

It didn't take Melinda long to realize that the mother deer had been shot, and this little one was her fawn. Had someone been hunting on their property, or had the doe been shot elsewhere and stumbled onto their land while it bled to death?

The fawn still hadn't moved but stood there with its nose and ears twitching. Melinda bent down and picked it up, noting that the little deer was lightweight and couldn't have been more than a few days old—probably born late in the year.

She hurried from the woods and entered the barn a short time later, where she settled the fawn in an empty stall. "I'll need to find one of my feeding bottles and get some nourishment into you right away," she said, patting the deer on top of its head.

She stepped out of the stall and closed the door, planning to check on the deer when she returned from work later that afternoon.

When Melinda arrived home shortly before supper time, she headed straight for the barn, and Papa Noah showed up a few minutes later. "What's that deer doin' in one of the horse's stalls?" he asked, pointing at the fawn asleep in the hay.

Melinda explained how she'd found the baby deer in the woods beside its dead mother.

"I thought I had made myself clear when I told you and Isaiah not to go there today," Papa Noah said with a frown.

"I'm sorry, but if I hadn't gone, this poor little deer would have died."

"But what if the person who shot the fawn's mother had been nearby and took another shot that might have hit you?"

Melinda could tell by the creases in Papa Noah's forehead that he was concerned for her welfare. "God protected me as well as this one," she said, motioning to the fawn.

"Jah, well, don't go to the woods again. At least not until hunting season is over."

She nodded in reply.

Papa Noah glanced around. "Where's your brother? Was he with you when you found the deer?"

"He went fishing over at Rabers' pond soon after breakfast."

"And he's not back yet?"

"I don't know. I don't see his pole." She pointed to the wall where Isaiah usually hung his fishing gear.

"It'll be getting dark in a few hours, and I don't like the idea of him being at the pond so late. Some crazy hunters could be out road hunting before dusk. That's when the deer start to move around again."

"Would you like me to go look for him?" Melinda offered. "I could take the horse and buggy."

Papa Noah shook his head. "If he's not here within the hour, I'll go after him myself."

Gabe leaned his gun against a tree and took a seat on a log. Soon the sun would be going down, then the deer would likely show themselves.

"Sure am glad I could get into the woods this afternoon," he said, leaning his head back and savoring the last few moments of full sunlight. He had decided to hunt in the wooded area to the left of Rabers' pond, which wasn't posted.

Gabe thought about Melinda and wondered if folks were respecting the NO HUNTING signs her stepfather had put around their place. *Sure hope Melinda has the smarts to stay out of the woods until hunting season is over. No telling what could happen if someone goes onto their property and ignores the signs Noah put up.*

He reached into his backpack, checking to be sure he had brought along enough ammunition. Everything seemed to be in order. Now all he needed was a nice-sized buck to step into the clearing. His folks would be pleased to have some deer meat on the table during the winter months.

A twig snapped, and Gabe leaped to attention. He was about to grab his gun when Isaiah Hertzler stepped out from behind a tree.

"What are you doing here?" Gabe hissed. "Don't ya know how dangerous it is to be in the woods during hunting season when you're not one of the hunters?"

Isaiah shrugged. "I ain't scared. I was on my way home from fishin' at the pond."

"Well, you should be scared, and you should have taken the road, not cut through the woods."

"Mind if I shoot your gun again?" Isaiah asked, eyeing the item in question.

"Not unless we get your daed's permission. I think it'd be best if you went straight home, don't you?"

Isaiah shrugged. "Guess so."

Gabe started to get up, but his backpack fell to the ground. He reached down to pick it up, and when he lifted his head again, he was shocked to see Isaiah holding his gun.

Before Gabe could open his mouth, the gun went off. A piercing pain shot through his left shoulder, and he toppled to his knees. Fighting to remain conscious, a wave of nausea coursed through Gabe's stomach.

"Gabe! Gabe, are you all right?" Isaiah dropped down beside him, his face a mask of concern. "I—I didn't mean to shoot you. I don't know how the gun went off."

"I know, I know, but I'm bleedin' real bad," Gabe said through clenched teeth. "I need something to put on the wound so I can apply pressure."

Isaiah pulled a hanky from his back pocket and handed it to Gabe. He balled it up and shoved it against his shoulder, wincing in pain. "You need to go for help, Isaiah. If I try to stand, I'll most likely pass out."

The boy blanched. "You're not gonna die on me, are you?"

Gabe moaned and tried to make his voice sound more convincing than he felt. "I think I'll live, but I need to go to the hospital. Run home and tell your daed what's happened. Ask him to get to a phone and call for help."

Gabe felt warm blood soak through the hanky and onto his fingers, and the world started to spin. "Hurry, Isaiah. Hurry, please."

The last thing Gabe remembered was a muffled, "I'm goin'," then everything went black.

Melinda had just stepped out of the barn when her little brother dashed into the yard yelling and waving his arms. "I shot Gabe! I shot Gabe!"

She rushed out to meet him, her heart hammering in her chest. "What do you mean, you shot Gabe?"

202

"He needs to go to the hospital. He may be bleedin' to death." Isaiah was clearly out of breath, and his cheeks were red and splattered with tears.

Melinda grabbed his shoulders and gave them a little shake. "Slow down once, take a deep breath, and tell me what happened."

"I—I was walkin' through the woods on my way back from Rabers' pond when I ran into Gabe," Isaiah panted. "I asked if I could shoot his gun, but he said no."

"Then what did you do?"

"When Gabe was bent over his ammunition bag, I picked up the gun." Isaiah's lower lip trembled, and more tears spilled onto his cheeks. "The gun went off, Melinda. I didn't mean for it to, but the next thing I knew, Gabe was lyin' on the ground, and there was blood oozin' out of his shoulder."

"Where is Gabe now?" Melinda said, trying to keep her voice steady.

"He's—he's still back in the woods. Sent me to get Papa and call for help."

As the metallic taste of fear sprang to her mouth, Melinda grabbed Isaiah's hand, and they dashed for the house.

twenty-five

Thankful to be alive, Gabe reached over and placed his Bible on the nightstand next to his hospital bed and closed his eyes. *You were looking out for me today, Lord Me and Isaiah both, and I thank You for that.*

He thought about what could have happened if Melinda's little brother, who obviously hadn't realized the gun was loaded, had pointed it at himself and accidentally pulled the trigger. Or this afternoon, some hunter in the woods could have shot Isaiah, mistaking him for a deer. The boy wasn't even wearing an orange vest or any bright colors.

The accident was more my fault than his. I never should have taught Isaiah how to shoot a gun. Leastways, not without his folks' permission. He's only twelve years old, not really ready for hunting yet.

Gabe clenched his fists, and a shooting pain sliced through his injured shoulder. *I shouldn't have left the safety off my gun, either. That was a careless thing to do, and it makes me wonder if I should even own a gun.*

Heavy footsteps told Gabe someone had entered the room, and his eyes snapped open. A middle-aged nurse with bright red hair strode toward his bed. "How are you feeling?" she asked.

"My arm's pretty sore, but at least I'm alive."

She slipped a thermometer under Gabe's tongue, then wrapped his good arm with the blood pressure band. "You're lucky that bullet went into your shoulder and not your chest. It could have been much more serious and required some lengthier hours in surgery than you went through."

Gabe merely nodded in reply, as it was hard to talk with a foreign object in his mouth.

A few minutes later, the nurse removed the blood

pressure apparatus and the thermometer. "Looks like your temperature is normal, and your pressure's right where it should be."

"When can I go home?"

"The doctor wants to keep you here overnight to watch for possible infection. If everything looks good by tomorrow morning, he'll probably release you then."

"Glad to hear it. I don't enjoy being in the hospital so much."

The nurse chuckled. "There are few that do." She nodded toward the door. "There's someone in the hall waiting to see you."

Gabe cranked his head in that direction. "Is it my folks? They were here earlier, but I told 'em to go home and get some sleep."

"It's not your parents, Gabe. It's a young Amish woman with blond hair and pretty blue eyes."

Gabe pushed himself to a sitting position as a mixture of excitement and dread coursed through his body. He was pretty sure the woman the nurse had described was Melinda, because his sisters all had dark hair, and he couldn't think who else might be here to see him.

Maybe I shouldn't see Melinda right now. She's most likely miffed and probably came here to give me a piece of her mind for allowing Isaiah to handle a gun again. Gabe glanced at the door. *'Course, I never said he could touch my gun, but he might not have if I hadn't shown him how to shoot in the first place.*

"Should I show the young woman in?" the nurse asked, breaking into Gabe's deliberations.

He nodded. "Might as well get this over with."

The woman raised one auburn eyebrow and looked at Gabe in a curious way, but then she shrugged and left the room. A few seconds later, Melinda entered, and her red face and swollen eyelids let Gabe know she had been crying.

"Are you all right?" they said at the same time.

Melinda smiled. "Jah, I'm fine. It's you I'm worried about."

She's worried about me. Now that's a good sign. Maybe she's not here to chew me out after all. Gabe nodded toward the chair. "Come, have a seat."

Melinda moved slowly across the room in a daze. It was hard to comprehend all that had happened this afternoon, and now here was Gabe lying in a hospital bed in Springfield, recovering from surgery during which the doctors had removed a bullet from his shoulder.

Melinda remembered how after Isaiah had come home and they'd called for help, he had led Papa Noah back to the woods where Gabe lay wounded, while she and Mama rode over to the Johnsons' place to use their phone and call for help. She had never been more frightened in her life, thinking she might not see Gabe again and begging God to save his life.

"Are you sure you're okay?" Gabe asked, pushing

Melinda's thoughts to the back of her mind. "Your face is as white as my bedsheets."

"I—I was just thinking how pale you looked when the ambulance took you away earlier today, and how scared I was of never seeing you again." She flopped into the chair with a groan. "Oh, Gabe, I'm glad you're going to be all right, and I'm ever so thankful God has answered my prayers."

"Me, too." He smiled at her in such a sweet way it was all Melinda could do to keep from throwing herself into his arms. But that wouldn't be a good idea, not with his injury and all. Besides, they needed to talk and get some important issues resolved.

"Melinda, I've made a decision—"

"Gabe, I need you to know something—"

They had both spoken at the same time.

"You go first," she prompted.

"No, that's okay. I'd like to hear what you've got to say."

Melinda reached out and took his hand, holding it gently and stroking her thumb back and forth across his knuckles.

"Umm . . . You're just what the doctor ordered," he murmured. "Better than any old shot for pain, that's for certain sure."

She cleared her throat and looked directly into his eyes. "Your accident has caused me to do some serious thinking."

Gabe nodded. "Same here."

"I don't want to spend the rest of my life without you."

"That goes double for me, Melinda."

She smiled, and relief flooded her soul. "I've come to the conclusion that even if I can't become a vet, and even if you continue to hunt, I want us to be together."

His eyes brightened. "Does that mean you still want to marry me?"

She nodded. "I've been praying and reading my Bible, and God showed me that family and friends, as well as my personal relationship with the Lord, are more important than anything else."

"I'm glad." Gabe smiled. "Now I have somethin' I'd like to say to you."

"What is it?"

"I've been layin' here in this hospital bed, prayin' and askin' God what I should do to make things right between us." He squeezed her hand. "For me, hunting should only be done whenever there's a real need—for food, I mean. I don't want to hunt just for the sport of it, the way some folks do."

"I think I could live with that, as long you don't shoot any of the deer I'm feeding."

"I wouldn't think of doing that," he said in a serious tone. "But I believe you'd better hear what else I have to say."

Melinda tipped her head. "What is it?"

Gabe drew in a deep breath. "I've decided that if becoming a vet is really that important to you, then I'll go English with you."

Melinda's mouth dropped open. "You—you would really do that for me?"

He nodded, and tears shimmered in his hazel eyes. "I've been miserable since our breakup, and I can't stand the thought of going through life without you at my side. I want to be with you, Melinda."

She shook her head. "No, Gabe, I thought that's what I wanted, but I can't ask you to make such a sacrifice."

Gabe nodded toward the Bible lying on the table beside his bed. "I'd like you to read something I read earlier. I marked the page with a slip of paper."

Melinda opened the Bible to the place he had marked and read the verse out loud. " 'Be ye therefore followers of God, as dear children.' " She paused and sniffed back the tears that threatened to spill over. "Oh, Gabe, I want to follow God all of my days; that's the most important thing."

"Jah. That's true for me as well."

"As much as I enjoy caring for sick and orphaned animals, I've been wrong to put it before my relationship with the Lord or those I love so much." Tears coursed down Melinda's cheeks, but she didn't bother to wipe them away. "I must learn to be content as I seek after God and try to do His will."

Gabe nodded. "But what if you could serve God and still take care of the animals that are so dear to you?"

"How can I do that without the proper training?"

"Since I woke up from surgery, I've been praying about everything," he said. "And I think God has given me an idea."

She leaned closer. "What is it?"

"After we are married, I'd like to make you more

cages—regular ones for the animals you would keep until time to let go, and larger ones, more like the critters' natural surroundings, for those who aren't able to be set free."

"Oh, Gabe, Grandpa Hertzler suggested something like that to me sometime ago, but I never mentioned it to you. If God gave you the same idea, it must be His will."

"And with the new cages, you could continue to care for animals the way you're doing now."

"But I still won't be able to help the animals who are seriously injured."

"You can turn those over to Dr. Franklin."

She nodded. "That's true. It doesn't have to be me who makes them well. Just as long as they have a place to stay while they're mending or needing a home because they're orphaned."

Gabe motioned her to come closer, and when she leaned her face near his, he kissed her tenderly. "I love you Melinda. Will you marry me?"

"Oh, jah. I'd be ever so pleased to be your Amish wife."

epilogue

Six months later

Melinda and Gabe stood side by side as family and friends gathered around to offer congratulations on their marriage, which had taken place only moments earlier. Melinda had never been happier. While she hoped to spend many days ahead caring for her animal friends, her primary goal would be to care for the man she loved so dearly.

Gabe's four sisters and their husbands and children were the first through the line, and Melinda was pleased when each one welcomed her into the family.

Aaron came through after that and congratulated them. Gabe smiled and patted his friend on the back. "You're the next one to be married, ya know."

Aaron shook his head. "No way!"

Gabe glanced over at Melinda and winked. "That's what they all say."

Aaron's face turned bright red, but he just smiled and moved on.

Melinda's family followed. "I left my gift for you on the table inside," Grandpa Hertzler said as he gave Melinda a hug. "It's a box filled with jars of my home-made rhubarb-strawberry jam." He winked at Gabe. "Melinda's mamm taught her how to make it, but I think mine's much better."

Melinda and Gabe laughed, and Melinda turned to embrace her aunt Susie.

"I'm so glad you decided not to leave home," Susie whispered in Melinda's ear. "It wouldn't be the same around here without you."

Melinda nodded. "I'm glad, too."

Isaiah was next, and he gave Melinda a quick hug, then turned to Gabe with a wide smile. "Sure am happy to have ya as my big brother. Maybe someday, when you think I'm old enough, we can go huntin' together."

Gabe glanced over at Melinda, as though needing her approval. She nodded and said, "Just as long as you don't hunt on our property."

"Wouldn't think of it," Isaiah and Gabe said at the same time.

Papa Noah and Mama followed Isaiah, and both offered hugs and congratulations to the happy couple. "When I was your age, I had recently left home," Mama whispered to Melinda. But I'm glad that my daughter has more sense than I had then."

Melinda wiped tears from her damp cheeks and gave her mother another hug. "But you came back home, and because of it, you married Papa Noah. That was a very *gluch* thing."

Mama nodded. "And now you're all grown-up and have married a wonderful man, which is also a smart thing."

"Jah, it took me awhile, but I finally realized that what I have right here is more important than any animal or anything the world has to offer."

Melinda's folks moved on, and Gabe's parents came next. Leah's eyes filled with tears as she hugged Melinda. "Take good care of my boy, okay?"

Melinda nodded. "I will. You can count on that."

"I have a wedding present for you that couldn't be put on the gift table," Gabe's daed said after he had hugged them both.

"Is it a new buggy horse?" Gabe asked with a chuckle.

Stephen shook his head. "It's somethin' I think you'll like even better."

"What is it?"

"I took care of some important paperwork the other day, and you are now the official owner of Swartz's Woodworking Shop."

Gabe's eyes grew large, and his mouth hung wide open. "You mean it, Pap?"

Stephen nodded. "Sure do. I'm sixty-five years old, and for some time I've been wantin' to take life a little easier. I'd like to spend more of my days fishin' and whittlin'. But of course I'll be available to help you in the shop whenever you need me."

Melinda could see by Gabe's strained expression that he was on the verge of tears. "I'll do my best to keep the place running smoothly, Pap. And I'd count it a privilege to have your help anytime."

When Gabe's daed moved away, Melinda reached up to stroke the side of her husband's clean-shaven cheek. She knew that since he was now a married man and would begin growing a beard right away, there wouldn't be many days left to touch the smooth skin on his face. But that didn't bother her so much. In fact, she'd always enjoyed the feel of Papa Noah's and Grandpa's fuzzy beards when they tickled her chin.

"You know what, Gabe?" she said as he stared lovingly into her eyes.

"What?"

"I have learned so many things in the last few

213

months, but there's one thing that stands out as the most important."

"And what might that be?"

"Like an obedient fawn follows its mother, I will always follow God, because I am his dear child. And as I follow God's leading, each day will be blessed because you will be at my side."

Gabe leaned down and brushed his lips across Melinda's forehead. "And you, my sweet *fraa,* will always be dear to me."

RECIPE FOR GRANDPA'S RHUBARB-STRAWBERRY JAM

Ingredients:
8 cups of rhubarb, cut into small pieces
4 cups of mashed strawberries
6 cups of sugar

Wash the fruit and cut the rhubarb into ½-inch pieces. In a large kettle, cover the rhubarb with half of the sugar and let it stand for 1 to 2 hours. Crush the berries and mix with the remaining sugar, then combine with the rhubarb. Place the mixture on the stove over low heat until the sugar dissolves, then boil rapidly, stirring often to prevent burning. Cook until the mixture thickens. Remove from heat, pour into sterilized canning jars, and seal while hot.

Center Point Publishing
600 Brooks Road ● PO Box 1
Thorndike ME 04986-0001 USA

(207) 568-3717

US & Canada:
1 800 929-9108
www.centerpointlargeprint.com